Sometimes, Molly thought, life was bizarre beyond words.

Here she was, plotting to seduce her own fiancé, and at the same time allowing another man to move into her house.

And not just any man, either.

A stud. A heartthrob. The Casanova of the pitch. A man who could take his pick of almost all the women in the western world. And quite frequently did.

Her fiancé would be appalled—that's if he even noticed.

Harlequin Presents® is proud to bring you
a brand-new trilogy from international
bestselling author

ANNE McALLISTER

Welcome to

The McGillivrays of Pelican Cay

Meet:
Lachlan McGillivray—he's ready to take his
pretend mistress to bed!
Hugh McGillivray—he's about to claim a bride…
Molly McGillivray—she's ready to surrender
to her Spanish lover!

Visit:
The stunning tropical island of Pelican Cay—
full of sun-drenched beaches,
it's the perfect place for passion!

The McGillivrays of Pelican Cay:
McGillivray's Mistress—November 2003 #2357
In McGillivray's Bed—July 2004 #2406
And Molly's story in *Lessons from a Latin Lover*

Anne McAllister

LESSONS FROM A LATIN LOVER

Pelican Cay

HARLEQUIN®

TORONTO • NEW YORK • LONDON
AMSTERDAM • PARIS • SYDNEY • HAMBURG
STOCKHOLM • ATHENS • TOKYO • MILAN • MADRID
PRAGUE • WARSAW • BUDAPEST • AUCKLAND

ISBN 0-373-12467-8

LESSONS FROM A LATIN LOVER

First North American Publication 2005.

Copyright © 2005 by Barbara Schenck.

This edition published by arrangement with Harlequin Books S.A.

® and TM are trademarks of the publisher. Trademarks indicated with ® are registered in the United States Patent and Trademark Office, the Canadian Trade Marks Office and in other countries.

www.eHarlequin.com

Printed in U.S.A.

CHAPTER ONE

THE TROUBLE with blinding flashes of inspiration, Molly Mc-Gillivray decided as she scowled into the innards of the ancient Jeep she was removing the carburetor from, was that they were never in one's comfort zone.

If they were, of course, they wouldn't *be* blinding flashes of brilliance. They would be "ho hum, yes, of course" notions that one would have thought of long ago.

The other trouble with blinding flashes of inspiration was that, once you thought of them, they wouldn't go away.

They were so outrageous, so perverse, so downright awful that you couldn't forget them!

They nagged and pestered and generally haunted you all the livelong day.

Like today.

Ever since her longtime fiancé, Carson Sawyer had come home last month, Molly had been wracking her brain for some subtle way to make him wake up and remember that they were, in fact, engaged.

Well, not exactly remember. She knew Carson remembered. It was *handy* to remember. Having a fiancée allowed him to keep his attention on business and kept the fortune hunters at bay. It was "useful" to be engaged, he'd once told her cheerfully. And back then she'd been quite happy to agree.

It had been useful to her, too.

But that was then. Enough was enough. They'd been engaged for years. It was time to *do* something about it—like get married.

Try telling Carson that.

Actually she had tried. But Carson's mobile phone had rung the first time she'd broached the subject. And he'd had an emergency appointment another time. And the last time he'd been home, well, he certainly hadn't noticed what she wanted him to notice—that they weren't getting any younger, that everyone else was married and having kids and it was time they did, too.

She didn't suppose things like starting a family were high on his list of priorities. She remembered well enough what her brother Hugh had said when she'd asked him what had attracted him to Syd, his wife.

"Sex," he'd said.

Syd had punched him.

"She's a great housekeeper, too," he'd added with a grin, dodging a second blow and then circling around to catch her in an embrace. "But I think it was mostly how unbelievably sexy she was." He'd nuzzled her ear. "Still is," he'd added with a wink, reaching down to pat her four-month-pregnant belly. Syd had rolled her eyes, but the light of love had been in them, and Molly knew the feeling was mutual.

It was true, Molly realized. Sex did play a part. A big part. And her sister-in-law had sex appeal in spades. Sydney had probably been born with a come-hither look in her eyes. Molly figured she'd been born with safety lenses over hers so she wouldn't get grit in them when she worked on engines which she did every day as the mechanic at Fly Guy Island Charters, the business she owned with Hugh.

Molly loved the business. She loved the engines. But men didn't notice women who worked on engines. Not as *women,* anyway.

And they certainly didn't have sexual fantasies about a woman who could take apart a carburetor and put it back together with no pieces left over. They didn't want to take

her to bed and make hot sweet love to her. They didn't want
to set a wedding date.

It didn't even occur to them. To him. To Carson.

So she needed help. She needed to get his attention. To
appeal to him on the same basic elemental level that Syd had
appealed to Hugh. She needed to become a sexy, alluring
woman.

Something of a stretch, she thought grimly, when she was
generally covered in motor oil and wearing her brother
Hugh's T-shirts and steel-toed boots.

But she was willing to work. She just didn't know where
to start.

Or she hadn't.

Until last night.

Last night she'd gone to the Grouper, the island's most
"happening" watering hole and had sat at one of the tables
by the wall, watching the "happenings"—all the flirting and
teasing and male-female innuendo stuff—trying to get an idea
of how to do it. From a distance she didn't have a clue.

All she'd seen was who was at the center of it all—Joaquin
Santiago.

Of course.

Molly grappled with the carburetor a little more fiercely
than was absolutely necessary, her jaw bunching as she remembered the moment the idea had entered her head.

She'd been sipping a beer and watching God's gift to
women, until recently one of Spain's most important exports
to the soccer world, Joaquin Santiago, assessing the females
who were attempting to charm him. An accident had ended
his career just months ago, and according to her other brother,
Lachlan, he was still feeling the effects of it. Molly, watching
him, couldn't see it had left any lasting effects at all.

It certainly hadn't done anything to dim his legendary appeal—or charm.

He smiled at this one, chatted with that one, flirted with
them, one and all. And then something happened. One woman

appeared to catch his attention. Molly saw him straighten, zero in. His wicked grin flashed. The devil-may-care glint in his eye was evident clear across the room as he focused on that one woman and cut her out of the crowd.

Like a cutting horse with a cow, Molly thought, having seen some Texans doing exactly that last weekend on the television.

As Molly watched, Joaquin's gaze locked with the woman's. They'd smiled. Flirted. They'd moved closer together as they talked. The others didn't leave, but it became clear they were a couple. Joaquin's hand lifted as he gestured. The grin flashed again, and when his hand came down it was on the woman's arm. She moved in closer.

Molly watched intently. Two tourists moved between her and the unfolding drama. She leaned sideways, practically tipping off the bar stool to get a better look. But it wasn't fifteen minutes until Joaquin and that night's conquest—or had she conquered him? Molly wondered—left the bar together.

Back to the Moonstone, undoubtedly, where she would share his bed.

Molly gave the wrench a vicious twist, and the nut came off and clanked to the floor. "Damn it!"

She scrabbled after it. Got it. Then pulled back and came up too soon, banged her head. She saw stars—and a vision of Joaquin with last night's blonde in his arms.

The night before that it had been a brunette. In the last week, Molly could recall half a dozen women she'd seen him with. Obviously, the man was a sex god.

But just as obviously, the women had something, too. What?

What caused a man to single one out? Hone in on her? Want her?

Ask him, her idiot brain had suggested. Right there in the middle of the Grouper the notion had come to her, and had almost knocked her on her butt.

Yeah, right, she'd countered her own idiocy. *Just walk up*

*to the playboy of the Western World and ask him what he
finds appealing about any given woman.*

For him they only had to be breathing.

But even as she thought it, she knew it wasn't true. Joaquin
had standards. He had his pick of women, and he only chose
certain ones.

"I'd take his leftovers," Hugh had said once in his pre-
Syd days.

Ask him, the voice persisted.

Molly snorted again, just thinking about it. Joaquin Santiago didn't even know she was alive.

Well, he knew. He was one of her brother Lachlan's best
friends in the world. He'd been in and out of her life ever
since he and Lachlan had played soccer together in Italy when
he was nineteen. Years later he'd come to Lachlan's wedding
and to Hugh's, bringing a different, equally gorgeous, French
model to each. He'd been charming to everyone, even Molly,
giving her a taste of the Santiago charm as he'd asked to be
introduced.

"Introduced?" Hugh had goggled. "That's Molly! In a
dress."

It had been almost funny to see the unflappably debonair
Santiago looking momentarily nonplussed as he'd had to admit he hadn't recognized Lachlan's sister wearing one of her
friend Carin Campbell's outfits.

"Dab a little engine grease on your nose, Mol'," Hugh had
suggested cheerfully. "Then he'll know you."

"Shut up." She'd laughed because she hadn't cared what
the likes of a playboy like Joaquin Santiago thought of her.
Still didn't.

She'd refused to dance with him then. She didn't want to
talk to him now. But clearly he knew what men found sexy
and alluring in a woman. He knew what made a man sit up
and take notice. He knew what made *him* sit up and take
notice.

Ask him, that irritating little voice in her head plagued her again.

But still she resisted. It would be too awful, too humiliating. How girly was it to admit you didn't even know how to act like a girl? Molly shuddered at the thought. She hated admitting any weakness. She'd spent her life determined to keep up with her two older brothers, and damn it, she had. Anything they could do, she could do better.

Almost.

There were some things, she was beginning to realize, that they would never have to do, blast their miserable hides.

She finished disassembling the carburetor and plunked the pieces in a pan of cleaner to soak. Surely she could come up with a better idea before Carson came home again.

It wasn't like he would be here anytime soon. She had assumed he would come to the Pelican Cay Homecoming Festival this month. It was going to be a big deal. It had been Syd's idea almost from the start. Working with Lachlan and Lord David Grantham, she had come up with a way of bringing ex-islanders home and enticing tourists to the island for a weekend of fun and revelry. Everyone on the island had got behind the plan, and Molly had thought Carson's return would be a given. But when she'd mentioned it, he'd shaken his head.

"Can't. Got to go to Ireland."

She'd smiled and done her best to hide her disappointment, telling herself he needed to do his job, and that it wasn't important. There would be time for them. Hadn't he just recently bought that big house in Savannah he was planning to restore? Didn't that mean he was thinking about marriage and family?

Maybe she didn't need to do anything to entice him.

Carson was a dark horse, after all. He kept his own counsel and did his own thing in his own time. No one else from Pelican Cay had gone from a poor fisherman's son to a multimillionaire in twelve short years. Carson had because he had always known what he wanted to do.

And he'd simply gone out and done it. He hadn't talked about it.

Perhaps next time he came, he wouldn't talk about marriage, either, he'd just bring a license and they'd get hitched.

Or perhaps he'd be as distracted as ever, Molly thought wearily.

The phone rang. She had gunk on her hands and let the answering machine get it. Whoever wanted to schedule a flight could leave a message and Hugh could call them when he got back.

"Mol'? Sorry I missed you. Thought you'd be there."

Oh, God! She stumbled across the room and punched the speaker button with her elbow. "Carson? Hi! I'm here! I've got oil, er…" She didn't need to spell it out for him. "Never mind. How are you? *Where* are you?"

"In Miami. Just got a break in a meeting. Just wanted to say I ran into a couple of islanders last night and we got to talking. Got a little homesick." There was a catch in his voice that made Molly smile.

"Really?"

"Yeah. Missed it. Missed you," he said gruffly. "God, it's so damn hectic all the time. The business. The house. Stuff… We never really got to talk last time I was home."

Molly's heart kicked over. "No," she said carefully. "But I knew you were busy."

"I was. Still am," he said. "But some things are more important, you know?"

"I know."

"Good. So I just wanted to let you know I've rescheduled Ireland. I'll be there for homecoming."

Molly grinned. "You will?"

"Yep. And we can talk and— Oh, hell. Gotta run."

"Carson—"

"Not now, Mol'. Can't talk. Sorenson's off the phone. I've

gotta go. We will, though. Promise. See you next Saturday.''
There was a click and Molly stood staring at the dead phone.

Outside she could hear the Pelican Youth Soccer team yelling as they practiced and her brother Lachlan shouted out
instructions for a drill. Inside she could hear the pounding of
the blood in her ears.

Carson was coming home!

A surge of hope shot through her, followed at once by the
tempering memory of his promise that they were ''going to
talk.''

Fine. Good. She wanted to talk. But she and Carson had
been talking for years. That's pretty much all they had ever
done beside some dreaming and some kissing and some teenage groping and fooling around. Everything else had been set
aside because Carson had been far too busy.

And because he'd never been especially inclined to make
love to a woman who smelled like engine oil and wore steel-
toed boots? Molly wondered.

Well, she could get rid of the smell and buy a new pair of
shoes.

And then what?

Joaquin Santiago would know, her irritating little voice reminded her.

And yes, that was true. He would. But she did *not* want to
ask him!

OF ALL THE PLACES ON EARTH Joaquin Santiago had been—
and he'd done his share of moving around in more than a
dozen years of playing professional soccer—he had always
liked Pelican Cay best.

He'd first visited the tiny Caribbean island at age nineteen
when he'd come to spend a holiday with his soccer teammate
Lachlan's family. It had seemed an idyllic lazy paradise to a
boy born and bred in the hustle and bustle of Barcelona. It
had been his bolt-hole ever since, the perfect getaway from
the demands of his fast-paced frenetic lifestyle.

Not that he hadn't loved that lifestyle, too. In those days he'd sat on the beach, relishing the quiet, yet always aware, whenever he'd stared east toward the horizon, that it was out there—his fame, his fortune, his ''fantastic foot'' which had made him one of the most feared strikers in football.

No longer.

For the past four weeks he had tried not to even look at the horizon. He knew what it held: nothing. It was empty. Distant. Barren. Bleak.

He had no future.

People hadn't forgotten him yet. It had only been five months, after all, since he'd been at the top of his game. Five months, one week and five days. If he thought about it, he could have come close to the number of hours since his accident, since he'd leaped up to head a ball at the same time as Yevgeny Pomasanov.

He'd hit the ball. Pomasanov's head had hit his. And his career had ended—just like that.

It was ridiculous. He still couldn't believe it. God only knew how many times he'd been hit in the head before Pomasanov's blow. Thousands, no doubt. It meant nothing, was an occupational hazard.

But this time it had been different. This time when he'd attempted to get up he couldn't. His arms, his legs didn't respond. He felt nothing. Couldn't move!

His brain still told his body what to do. But it was as if the connection had been severed. Unreal. *Unthinkable!*

He was young. In his prime! Soccer was his life!

But life as he'd known it for thirty-three years was over. They'd taken him off the field on a stretcher in a neck brace. For four days he'd lain in the hospital, paralyzed, motionless, as doctors hovered and poked and prodded. He'd felt nothing but an occasional tingling sensation and a desperate sense of panic.

The sports pages and tabloids had been full of speculation. Would he move again? Would he walk? Would he play?

Of course he would. He had to!

Life had always been about soccer. Soccer was what had saved him from having to spend his life in the mind-dulling Santiago family business. Of course he knew that one day it would be his destiny, but not right away. Not yet!

He loved soccer. He couldn't imagine doing anything else.

So the morning that the tingling sensations in his fingers and toes actually led to his moving them, he'd breathed an enormous sigh of relief. If he could move, he could come back.

It was just a matter of time. After all, he'd been hurt before. Three years ago he'd lost his spleen as a result of a motorcycle accident. He'd nearly died from loss of blood before the injury was discovered. But he'd recovered from that. He'd come back. And this time would be no different.

He'd worked his tail off. He'd done everything the docs told him to—and more. He'd rehabbed until he was sure he was as fit as ever. It had taken him four months. Then, a month ago, he'd walked into the training room and said to the docs, the trainers, the team owners, "I'm back. I'm as good as new. I can do everything I ever did."

And he went out onto the pitch and showed them.

They had watched politely. And then, to his amazement, they had shaken their heads. "You've recovered wonderfully," they agreed. "But you can't play soccer. It's too risky."

"What?" He'd stared at them, disbelieving.

"Spinal stenosis—" the congenital narrowing of the spine that had contributed to his paralysis and which they had discovered while treating him "—is nothing to mess around with. Next time you might not recover feeling at all."

"How do you know there will be a next time?" he'd demanded.

They'd just looked at him. "How do you know there won't?"

He'd argued. Damn it, he'd had to argue!

But in the end, it was the insurance companies who carried the day. They wouldn't insure him. It all came down to liability. Joaquin Santiago was too big a risk for any team.

Ergo, he couldn't play.

His world collapsed. He felt fine. He felt fit. He felt gutted. His father expected him to come back to Barcelona and get on with life.

"There's nothing wrong with you," Martin Santiago had said. "You just need something to do. A job," he'd added pointedly, "which has been waiting for you for fourteen years."

But Joaquin couldn't face it. Not yet.

"Take your time," his old teammate Lachlan McGillivray advised. "I know it feels like the end of the world. It felt like it to me when I retired. You get over it," he promised. "You just need some space while you find something else to do with your life."

Easy for Lachlan to say. Lachlan had long ago found something he wanted to do. He'd begun buying property and rebuilding and restoring old buildings, turning them into a series of one-of-a-kind small elegant inns across the Caribbean. Since retirement he'd made his home here on Pelican Cay where he'd married a local girl and had a baby son. His future, even out of soccer, was of his own making.

Joaquin's was not.

His future had always been a given. Soccer had given him a reprieve, but his life had been foreordained since birth. Santiago men went into the family business. It was as simple as that. For the past five generations all of them had devoted their lives to the company Joaquin's great-grandfather, for whom he'd been named, had begun.

Since there had been telephones, the Santiagos had been involved in communications. The company had evolved with the times, and now had its corporate fingers in a lot of pies. It was thriving, growing, facing daily challenges.

"Santiago men always faced the challenge," Martin was fond of saying.

Joaquin would, too. He knew that. His father expected it. So did he. Martin had been tolerant of the years Joaquin had spent playing soccer only because he was a strong vigorous man in good health who didn't need his only son and heir trying to take over before he was ready.

"So you play a while," his father had said, waving a hand dismissively.

But it had always been understood between them that when Joaquin's soccer-playing days were over, Santiagos was waiting and real life would start.

Joaquin was no fool. He'd always known he wouldn't play forever. He'd accepted that.

But that had been when "real life" was somewhere in the future. Not now.

Not yet.

But with one blow *yet* had become *now*. His father and the business were waiting. His mother with her lineup of prospective brides—more "real life"—was waiting.

But he couldn't face it.

He had been back in Barcelona two days when he knew he needed more time.

"I just need to get my head together," he'd told his father. "I need a little space before I start."

"Space? You've had four months!" Martin sputtered.

But his mother, Ana, the more patient of his parents, had taken his side. She'd patted his hand and said to his father, "Give him time, Martin. A month. Two. What's the difference after we have waited all these years. He needs to grieve for what he has lost."

His father had been skeptical, but in the end he'd agreed. "We will be waiting, though," he'd said giving Joaquin a stern, expectant look.

And Joaquin had nodded. "I know. I'll be here."

"Of course he will," his mother had said. "And then we

will all be happy and Santiagos will be waiting and—'' she'd kissed his cheek ''—finally you will get around to giving me those grandchildren I've been waiting for!''

That was the other half of his future—getting a mother for the inevitable Santiago offspring.

His mother had shaken her head with bemused tolerance at all the groupies who'd trailed after him during his soccer career. She didn't take them seriously. They were silly and transitory.

None of them would become ''the Santiago Bride.'' She knew that. So did Joaquin.

''Time enough for you to find the right woman when you are done playing games,'' she'd always said.

Something else to look forward to, he thought grimly now as he lay on the chaise longue on the small balcony outside his room at Lachlan's trendy Moonstone Inn and tried not to think about it.

He'd been here over three weeks now, every day trying to psyche himself up for his new life.

He wasn't there yet.

Listlessly he picked up the book he'd been trying to read for the past hour. Lachlan's wife, Fiona, had told him he'd love it.

''It's a real page turner,'' she'd assured him. But he'd been on the same one now for what seemed like a week. The words made no sense.

Weary, he lifted his gaze and stared across the water at the empty horizon.

''You *read?*'' The sudden sound of an astonished female voice made him jump.

He turned his head and saw Lachlan's grubby sister, Molly, standing on the balcony of the room next door.

He lifted a brow. ''Are they keeping engines in the guest rooms now?''

Molly was the mechanic at Fly Guy, Hugh McGillivray's island charter service. She was also a pilot, occasionally taking charters when Hugh was otherwise committed, but most of the time she was eyebrows deep in some greasy engine on a plane, boat, helicopter or motor vehicle.

Not, Joaquin thought, your average girly girl.

Probably the only one in the world who didn't even own a dress! A fact he had learned when he hadn't recognized her at Lachlan's wedding because she'd actually been wearing one. A borrowed one. But he hadn't known it at the time. He'd thought she was simply a fresh female face. She certainly hadn't looked like herself. On the contrary, she'd looked…pretty. Sexy.

Approachable. For once.

His mistake.

He'd felt foolish for not realizing who she was, but he'd got past it and had attempted to redeem himself by asking her to dance.

"Dance?" She'd stared at him, sounding incredulous. "With you?"

"I don't normally ask women to dance with someone else," he'd said stiffly.

She'd laughed, but it had been a forced laugh. And then she'd shaken her head. "Well, thanks, but no thanks. Don't put yourself out." And she'd turned away to talk to someone else!

Cheeky brat.

And the only woman who had ever turned him down.

Not that he gave a damn. There were far more fish in the sea. He hadn't spared her another thought. And he'd barely seen her since he'd been back. Oh, maybe they'd been in the same social gathering a handful of times because he was Lachlan's friend and she was Lachlan's sister.

But she was usually far too preoccupied with her engines even to deign to speak to him. And he had no desire to talk to her. He considered ignoring her now. And he might have, but at the moment even grubby tomboy Molly McGillivray was more welcome than his own dark thoughts.

"What are you doing over there?" he asked her.

"Suzette asked me to put some flowers in the room."

Lachlan's office manager and second in command, was all spit-and-polish efficiency. Joaquin couldn't imagine she'd let Molly—wearing her grimy work shorts, faded orange T-shirt, and oil-streaked bandanna wrapped around her forehead to tame a riot of coppery curls—anywhere near one of the Moonstone's pristine guest rooms. "Good thing she didn't ask you to bring clean towels." He grinned at the flash of green fire in Molly's eyes, then when something else seemed to flicker in them, he added, "*Lo siento.* I'm sorry. I just couldn't see Suzette sending you like—" he waved a hand in the direction of her grease-stained clothes "—that."

"I was coming up, anyway," Molly said stiffly.

"Oh." He expected she'd do whatever it was she'd come up for and leave, but she didn't. She stood there, so deep in thought she was making faces as she stared at him.

He frowned. "What?"

"Nothing." She hesitated, then glanced toward the door that led from his balcony into his room. "Is she gone?"

"Is who gone?"

"The flavor of the night. Whoever you brought back with you last night."

Joaquin stared at her. "What do you know about who I brought back with me last night?" he asked.

In point of fact he hadn't brought anyone back. He'd considered it. He'd even gone so far as to leave the Grouper with a pretty blonde tourist from Germany. But she'd giggled too much. He'd walked on the beach with her, then remembered a "pressing phone call" he needed to wait for. She'd offered to wait with him, "to keep him busy while he was waiting," she'd said with several more giggles. But he'd declined.

"I don't know anything about her," Molly said. "I just didn't want her to come waltzing out in the middle of—" she broke off.

Joaquin lifted a brow. "In the middle of...?" He gave her an expectant look.

She made more faces. Then she shifted from one foot to the other and seemed to almost balance on her toes. She reminded him of Lachlan poised in goal, anticipating, ready.

For what?

No clue. She seemed to be poised on the brink of some great statement which she somehow couldn't manage to get out. Well, if it had anything to do with disapproval of how he lived his life, she could take her opinions and stuff them!

"I need to talk to you," she blurted at last. Her face was red, and not entirely from the sun, Joaquin didn't think. Curious.

"Talk to me? About what?"

More faces. She balled her fingers into fists. "It's complicated," she said at last. She didn't look at him.

"Complicated how?"

"Look," she said fiercely with another suspicious glance at the door. "Is she in there or not?"

"There's no one in my room," Joaquin told her. He rose lazily and stood looking at her. "So if you'd like to go in..." he added, his voice laced with a lazy teasing innuendo.

If she could make innuendoes about his love life, he could do the same about hers.

. "No!" She gulped air. "I don't. I need—" She stopped again and looked almost anguished.

He'd never seen Molly McGillivray anguished. She'd always been cheerful and blunt and basically a sort of no-nonsense girl. "Is something wrong?" he asked her.

"No." She took a breath. "I just...have a proposition for you."

His eyes widened. "A *proposition?*"

What the hell did *that* mean?

"A *business* proposition," Molly said. Her voice sounded raspy and she licked her lips as if they were parched. She looked hot. The Caribbean sun was baking.

"Why don't you come over and sit down and tell me what you have in mind," Joaquin said. *Before you faint and fall off the damn balcony.*

"I—all right." She scrambled over the railing to his balcony, leaving a couple of greasy fingerprints on the white paint.

"Sit down," Joaquin said. If she had engine grease on the seat of her shorts that was Lachlan's problem. She was his sister, after all. "Do you want something to drink? Beer? A glass of wine? A soda?" There was a small but well-stocked refrigerator in his room.

"A beer," Molly decided abruptly.

And before he could make a move to get one for her, she darted past him into his room and got one herself! Actually she got two and handed one to him.

"Thank you," he said, deadpan.

She gave a jerky little nod. "My pleasure. Well, Lachlan's actually," she corrected herself. She twisted the cap off the beer as she paced around the small balcony, still not looking his way.

Joaquin watched, not speaking as she stopped with her back to him and stared out across the beach. Then she tipped her head back and took a long gulp of the beer before squaring narrow shoulders and turning to face him.

"I want to hire you," she said.

"Hire me?" His gaze narrowed. He didn't know the first thing about engines. Wasn't in the slightest bit interested in them. Never had been. And just because Lachlan had been saying he should stay busy, that didn't mean he needed some misguided female in steel-toed boots offering him work out of pity.

"No, thanks," he bit out.

Molly's fingers tightened on the beer bottle. "You haven't even heard me out."

"I don't need to. I don't know an oil pan from a tail rotor and I don't want to."

"I imagine even you could tell the difference between those two," she retorted with a roll of her eyes. But then she hunched her shoulders. "It's not that kind of work. It's something you're good at."

"Not soccer," he said flatly. "I'm not helping Lachlan with the soccer team."

In a misguided attempt to cheer him up when he'd first arrived, Lachlan had invited him to help coach the kids' soccer team. That was the last thing Joaquin wanted to do.

If he couldn't play the sport he loved, he wanted nothing at all to do with it. It hurt too much to watch anyone do what he could do no longer. Especially when he was going to be doing what he didn't want to do at all.

But Molly shook her head. "Not soccer."

Joaquin couldn't think of anything else he was good at. "Then what?"

Her fingers strangled the beer bottle again. She took a breath. "I need you to teach me—" another swift deep breath. And another. Hell, in a minute she'd hyperventilate! "—how to seduce a man."

His jaw dropped. The beer bottle slipped from his hand.

"Oh, for heaven's sake!" Molly bent down and snatched the bottle off the deck, slapped it on the table, then ducked past him into the room and, returning with one of the bathroom towels, used it to blot up the beer with a gravity far exceeding the amount that had spilled.

His brain was still buzzing, wondering if it was the heat of the afternoon sun or the beer that had caused his hearing to go. "You want me to *what?*"

As she mopped he could see that the back of her slender neck was almost as red as her hair. And when she stood up, her face was flaming. "Never mind! Forget I said anything. It was a stupid idea!" She tried to dart past him into the room, but he hauled her up short.

She jerked her arm, but he wouldn't let her go. "Sit down." He still couldn't believe it, but her behavior was making it seem more and more like his hearing wasn't as bad as he'd thought.

"Did you say you want me to teach you to—" now *he* was having trouble getting his mouth around the words! "—*seduce* a man?"

Her shoulders lifted and her mouth twisted in one of those distasteful faces she'd been making earlier. But then she met his gaze squarely and seemed to defy him to make something of it. "Yes." The word hissed through her teeth.

Good lord. He tried to bend his mind around it. His mind wasn't that flexible. "Why?" he asked stupidly.

"For the usual reasons," she snapped. "Why the hell do you think?"

He shrugged helplessly. He'd always thought he understood women very well. He sure as hell didn't understand this one!

She sighed and squared her shoulders beneath the gargantuan T-shirt, then said evenly, "Look. It's simple. I'm thirty-one years old."

He was surprised. Of course she had to be, as she was only a couple of years younger than he was. But somehow he'd never thought of her as any older than when he'd first met her. She'd been about seventeen then. Still, "Thirty-one?" he echoed doubtfully. "Are you sure?"

"Of course I'm sure! I'm not ancient."

"I know that," he said quickly. "I thought...younger. You look—"

"Like a thirteen-year-old boy?" Her mouth twisted.

Yes, actually. In those clothes. Though she sure as hell hadn't at Lachlan's wedding in that borrowed dress. But he wasn't going there, either. "Fine," he said at length. "You're thirty-one. So what? Like you said, it's not ancient."

"Not yet. But it's time I got married."

"Married?"

He'd never even seen her with a boyfriend! It wasn't that he'd thought she might prefer women, it was that she'd never given any indication of preferring anyone at all. Some people didn't.

"Not everyone has to get married," he said, in case she had suddenly begun to worry about it. "Lots of people lead perfectly happy single lives."

"You, for example," she said tartly. "I know that. But I presume that's because you want to."

"Damn right."

"So, fine. Hooray for you. But I *don't* want to."

He blinked at her vehemence. "You don't?"

"No!" She took a quick breath, then said more moderately, "No. I don't. As surprising as it may seem, I want a husband. I want a family. I always have." She said the words with almost as much bluntness as he was accustomed to hearing from her. And yet they weren't disinterested. There was an emotional edge underlying them. She sounded vulnerable.

Molly McGillivray? *Vulnerable?*

"Your sister wears army boots?" he'd said incredulously to Lachlan the first time he'd met her.

And Lachlan had agreed with a wince as he'd rubbed his shin. "And she knows how to use them."

That was the Molly McGillivray he knew. Not this one.

Now he rubbed the back of his neck and tried to think. The very notion of him helping some girl with marriage on her mind boggled his. *Marriage* wasn't even a word in his active vocabulary, despite his mother's recent not-so-subtle hints.

When it came to staying power, his romances—if indeed anyone beyond tabloid journalists dared call them that—rarely lasted longer than the half life of a loaf of bread. Which was the way he liked it.

In the past three weeks, he'd flirted with dozens of women and been delighted to have them flirt with him. Someday he would doubtless marry and do his duty by the family name.

But he was in no hurry. None at all.

Besides, what did seduction have to do with marriage? Unless Molly was planning to seduce some man, then kidnap him and haul him to the altar. He gave her a narrow assessing look.

"You want me to teach you how to nab some unsuspecting tourist?"

"Of course not!"

"Well, then—"

"He's not an unsuspecting tourist!"

"You've got someone in mind?"

"Of course."

"You do?" He couldn't keep the astonishment out of his voice. His mind darted to all the eligible men on the island. "Um…anyone I know?"

"I don't think you've met him. We grew up together. He lives in Savannah now—and elsewhere. His name is Carson Sawyer."

No, Joaquin hadn't met him. But he'd heard the name. Carson Sawyer was the "local boy who made good."

"You think *we're* driven to succeed?" Lachlan had once said to him when they were working their butts off. "You should meet Carson."

Carson Sawyer, last Joaquin had heard, was worth about as much as a small Mediterranean country.

And *this* was the man Molly had set her sights on?

Talk about aiming for the moon!

"I don't think—"

"We're engaged."

"*You and Carson Sawyer?*" Joaquin couldn't have disguised his shock if his life had depended on it. Tomboy Molly with all her rough edges and a hotshot, fast-track business tycoon like Carson Sawyer?

But Molly was nodding seriously. "Since I was fourteen and he was fifteen. Since he went to sea."

"That's—" Joaquin did the math in his head "—seventeen years ago!"

Molly shrugged. "We weren't in any hurry. It was right. We knew it. And we both had other things to do."

"But—"

"We were both happy," she insisted. "It worked. For both of us. We both did what we wanted to do. But now—" she lifted her shoulders "—now it's time."

"To seduce him?" His mind still wasn't that flexible.

"Haven't you been listening to anything I said?" she demanded.

"Yes, of course. It just seems a little, um…bloodless? Cut-and-dried?" Joaquin was bilingual, but he would have had trouble with this in any language at all.

"Exactly," Molly agreed, surprising him. Then she went on. "That's the point. It shouldn't be 'bloodless.' It should be wonderful, moving, passionate." Molly's voice became animated, the color rose in her cheeks again. She looked eager and alive and hopeful. And then, as quickly as it had come, her eagerness vanished and her shoulders slumped. "Only it isn't happening."

"It?"

"The passion. The…sex stuff."

She didn't want him to teach her about sex, did she? God almighty!

"He treats me like his pal. Which I am, of course," Molly said hastily. "But he needs to see me in a new light. So I—thought maybe you could help me."

He opened his mouth. Stood there. Stunned. Then closed it again.

"You are good at it," Molly said firmly. "I've seen you. *Lots* of times."

"Seen me what?" he demanded, visions of her spying on his bedroom activities making him decidedly uncomfortable.

"Pick up women. Get picked up by them. Flirt with them. You know," she said a little desperately. "I'm not good at that stuff. But I can learn," she added.

He looked at her doubtfully. "You want me to teach you how to seduce your boyfriend?"

"Fiancé. Why not? It's how I learned to repair engines. It's how I learned to fly. I went to an expert."

"I thought Hugh taught you to fly."

"I'm *not* asking Hugh to teach me how to seduce Carson! And I'm not asking Lachlan, either, so don't even suggest it!" Abruptly Molly headed for the wall to climb over it and leave. "Never mind. Forget it. I shouldn't have bothered. I should have known you'd think it was stupid." She turned on him. "If you say one word—"

"I'm not saying anything." He caught her arm again and swung her around so that she landed on the chaise and stared up at him. He stood over her, breathing hard, aware of a sudden new energy pumping through him. "Don't be so damn quick to jump to conclusions. What do you need to know?"

"If I knew I wouldn't be asking, would I?" Molly folded her arms across her chest. "I just want to make him look at me differently when he comes for the island homecoming. I want him to see me as a woman. He never has."

"Never?"

"Well, not never. But not for a while. We had things to do. We didn't want to just get married and have babies. So we got engaged. It took the pressure off."

"It did?" Joaquin shook his head, dazed at the logic. "How?"

"I didn't have to worry about finding a boyfriend, and he didn't have to worry about finding a girlfriend. We had each other, but we could go ahead and do our own things. Then someday, when the time was right, we'd get married. But he's so busy, he doesn't remember."

"So why haven't you reminded him?"

"I'm not begging Carson to marry me! He's got to want to. And he will," she said stoutly. "I just need to make him sit up and take notice. But I don't quite know where to start. That's where you come in. I can pay you."

"I don't want your damn money!"

"Well, too bad. I'm not a charity case!"

"No. You're a nutcase! How much time do you have to turn into a femme fatale?"

"Ten days."

"Ten days? That's all?"

Molly's chin lifted. "If you're any good, that should be long enough!"

"Or if *you* are," he countered.

She didn't flinch. Much.

They glared at each other. All he could see were her deep-green eyes, her face full of freckles, the smudge of oil on her nose and that grubby bandanna covering her forehead. For the first time in a month, he couldn't even see the emptiness of the horizon.

"It's a deal," he said. "I'll do it."

CHAPTER TWO

IT WAS QUITE POSSIBLY the stupidest thing she'd ever done.

Once she was back home, staring in the bathroom mirror as she stripped off her grimy shorts and T-shirt to take a shower, Molly even said so out loud.

"Stupid," she told herself. "Daft. Insane. You are a complete whacko. All of the above."

She still couldn't believe she had actually asked Joaquin Santiago to teach her to seduce a man. Even less could she believe he'd said yes.

Though if she thought about it, maybe that wasn't so hard to believe. It was no skin off his ego, after all, if she was too dim to even grasp the fundamentals. *He* wasn't the one who was going to look like an idiot.

The very thought of it made her shudder. In fact it made her feel more naked than she was, stepping into the shower right now.

But the truth was, she was desperate. The realization that things were changing had crept up on her slowly, beginning nearly two years ago when Lachlan's relationship with Fiona had almost ended in disaster.

Everyone could see how right they were for each other. And yet they almost hadn't made it happen. Lachlan had very nearly blown it.

Still, she'd assured herself then, that was Lachlan. Her oldest brother had always been totally focused on the soccer pitch and totally clueless in real life. But then sane, sensible Hugh had nearly screwed things up, too, when he'd let Sydney get away!

It had taken him *months* to find her. And he was damned lucky, to Molly's way of thinking, that Syd loved him as much as she did.

Both her brothers had been incredibly lucky. They'd come to their senses before it was too late. But some people didn't.

Hugh's first love, Carin, and her husband, Nathan, for example, had stayed apart for years after their first encounter. And Nathan's brothers, according to the island telegraph, had had their own relationship problems.

The path to true love, she knew all too well, was fraught with peril. So it made good sense to make sure the same thing didn't happen to her and Carson. The thought had been growing ever since Lachlan's marriage. It had come into sharper focus after Hugh's wedding. But it hadn't taken on a real sense of urgency until Duncan appeared.

Duncan was an absolute dreamboat. He was, without a doubt, the most gorgeous male Molly had ever set eyes on. He had eyes as blue as the sea, a dimple in his left cheek that begged to be touched, and a smile so teasing and engaging that every woman he flashed it at nearly swooned at the sight.

And he was only four months old.

The boy would be a lady-killer when he grew up.

One look at Duncan Dunbar McGillivray, her drop-dead-gorgeous nephew, and Molly had fallen like a ton of bricks. Every maternal instinct she'd ever buried beneath engine grease and motor oil and a baseball cap was suddenly on alert.

She caught herself chucking him under the chin and tickling his toes and playing peek-a-boo. She hummed long-forgotten lullabies while she cleaned carburetors, and snatches of old nursery rhymes ran through her head while she welded metal frame.

"Who the hell is the Grand Old Duke of York?" Hugh had demanded last week. "Don't tell me Grantham got promoted."

Lord David Grantham hadn't—and never would—ascend to a dukedom. "No. Dave's still Dave, as far as I know," Molly had mumbled, embarrassed, then clamped her lips together and tried not to think in rhyme the rest of the afternoon.

But she still volunteered to baby-sit without being asked. She bought stuffed dogs and school-of-fish mobiles and cardboard books by the dozen. She relished every smile Duncan bestowed on her and cherished every bubble he blew and every noise he made.

That she was such a sap when it came to babies astonished her. She'd always liked kids. She'd been a teacher for several years before she'd decided she'd rather be a mechanic. But this wasn't just "liking kids"; this was different.

This was *Duncan*. With eyes like his father's and a nose like his grandma's and a glimmer of his mother's—or his auntie Molly's—red in his hair, in Duncan Molly saw hints of the children that someday she might have. And she found herself rocking him and imagining the day when she would rock a child of hers and Carson's.

In the region of her heart, she began to feel pangs she'd never ever felt before.

And that was when she knew she and Carson had waited long enough. Carson had made plenty of millions. She had a job she loved. Their engagement had served its purpose. She wanted more.

She couldn't say Carson felt the same.

The last time he'd come home, eager to show off her nephew, Molly had taken the baby with her to meet him. She was sure he'd take one look at this wonderful new human being and would instantly understand.

He'd been...surprised...to say the least.

"Who's this?" he'd asked. It had been seven months since he'd been home, so Molly supposed he might not have known Fiona was expecting. But surely just looking at Duncan, he would know.

But before she could reply, he'd gone on, "Are you trying

to tell me something, Mol'?'' And then he'd shrugged and said a little ruefully, "You could have just told me you'd found somebody else."

And then she'd realized Carson had completely misunderstood, that he thought Duncan was *hers!*

"Duncan is my nephew! He's Lachlan and Fiona's. I would never—I'm engaged to *you!*"

A relieved grin had spread over Carson's hard handsome face. "Well, that's all right then," he'd said cheerfully and looped an arm over Molly's shoulders. "How come you've got him?"

"Fiona's sculpting this afternoon. I said I'd baby-sit."

He'd looked dismayed. "I thought maybe we'd go fishing."

His reaction had definitely not been all that she had hoped for. But Molly supposed she shouldn't have been surprised. Carson hadn't been expecting to see her with a baby. But if she'd hoped the notion would grow on him, it hadn't.

He'd been distracted, preoccupied with business, going back and forth to talk to Tom Wilson at The Lodge on the private island just south of Pelican Cay. They had "irons in the fire," he told Molly. Something to do with another retreat center for burned-out execs in Savannah like the one Tom had already established at The Lodge. Carson had been helping him with the Savannah operation.

It was Tom, in fact, who had rung up the evening she'd actually tried to steer the conversation around to their engagement and—maybe someday—marriage.

But she'd barely got into it when Tom had rung. Carson had said, "Can't talk now," and had gone off to talk shop.

"We'll do it later," he'd promised Molly.

But there hadn't been time.

Well, at homecoming there would be. Time for talk—and considerably more than that, Molly vowed as she scrubbed vigorously under the shower's spray. Provided she didn't die of mortification from Joaquin Santiago's "seduction lessons" first.

He had told her he'd "be in touch," when she'd left his room at the Moonstone.

"When?" she'd asked. Given a specific time, she figured she could gear herself up for the experience. Or think of a reason to chicken out.

"I need to think about it," he'd said.

"Really?" She'd been surprised actually. "You mean it's not instinctive."

"We'll see, won't we?" he'd said with that smooth, seductive voice that could send shivers down a woman's spine.

She'd done her best to look indifferent. "I guess. But I'm going to the Grouper tonight if you want to do it there," she said with what she hoped was more nonchalance than she felt. The minute he'd agreed she'd felt a frisson of panic, of having jumped into the deep end. And the feeling wasn't going away. On the contrary it was getting worse.

Maybe she wouldn't go to the Grouper tonight. Maybe she'd just stay home.

Or maybe he wouldn't be there. Maybe, she thought with some degree of hope, he'd change his mind.

On that heartening note, she shut off the shower. Just as well, as the water was beginning to run cold. She snagged a towel and scrubbed at her hair when she heard a knock on the door.

"Oh, cripes." She'd forgotten Fiona had said she might come by with Duncan. "Come on in," she called through the high open window. "I'll be right out."

She rubbed her hair until it stuck out all over her head, ran her fingers through it to tame it slightly, then wrapped the towel saronglike around her and skittered down the stairs to see her favorite nephew.

"Hey!" she beamed, prepared to sweep Duncan into her arms.

"Hey yourself." Joaquin was standing in the living room looking as if he'd never seen a woman in a towel before.

Molly wanted to drop through the floor. "What are you doing here?" she demanded, hot with embarrassment.

"Someone...you—" he clarified pointedly "—said 'Come on in.' So I did."

"I didn't mean you!"

"No? But then you must be in the habit of inviting unknown persons into your house while you cavort around in a state of undress," he said.

"I thought you were Fiona and Duncan!"

"I'm not."

"I can see that. Go outside."

"I don't think so." He'd recovered from his astonishment and was eyeing her with considerable interest. It was making her even hotter.

"It's rude to stare," Molly said irritably.

A sudden grin slashed across his tanned face. "Not necessarily," he said. "Not if I'm awestruck by your beauty."

Molly snorted. "Pull the other leg while you're at it."

"Pull your leg?" He looked intrigued and moved toward her as if he were going to do just that.

Molly hopped back up on the steps. "Stop that! And don't pretend you don't know what it means. You know exactly what it means. You speak English perfectly. You even sound like a Texan sometimes."

"My mother's influence," he agreed, still eyeing her, still moving closer.

Molly clutched the banister, refusing to allow herself to edge farther back up the stairs.

"Tell me," He cocked his head and regarded her speculatively. "Have you ever greeted Carson in a towel?"

"Of course not!"

"Maybe you should. Solve all your problems." His grin flashed.

Molly frowned. "Very funny. What are you doing here? I suppose you've had second thoughts."

"I certainly am now," he murmured so softly she wasn't sure she heard him.

"What did you say?"

"Nothing." He cleared his throat and dragged his gaze from the length of her legs past the skimpy towel up to her face. "I came to invite you out for a drink."

"What? A drink?" she said stupidly.

He nodded. "Will you come with me for a drink at the Grouper?"

"I already told you I was going to the Grouper," she reminded him.

"Sí." He smiled as if she were missing the point. "But now I am inviting you. For a lesson." The smile took on a decidedly worrying aspect.

Molly swallowed. "I don't know," she said hastily.

"Do you want to seduce your man or not?"

"I already said I did! But I don't see what inviting me out for a drink has to do with it."

"No, you don't. But then," he said affably, "if you knew what you were doing you wouldn't have asked me, would you, *querida?*"

Molly knew enough Spanish to know what *querida* meant. "Stop using endearments!" she snapped.

He made a tsking sound. "Ah, Molly. Are you perhaps the one who is having second thoughts?"

Heavy-lidded eyes so dark they were almost black bored into hers. There was an intensity in them she'd never seen in Carson's. Or in any man's, come to think of it.

Molly's mouth went dry. She couldn't look away. She pressed her lips together and shook her head fiercely. "No!"

He smiled, a supremely satisfied smile. "Then would you like to have a drink at the Grouper with me?" He paused a beat. A black eyebrow lifted as he waited. When she still couldn't manage a word, her brain cells scattered like marbles, he prompted her. "Say 'Yes, thank you, Joaquin.' And smile. First lesson."

Molly didn't smile. She stood, grim-faced and desperate, wondering what she was getting herself into. She wanted to know what to do with Carson! She wanted a future with him and with little dark-haired blue-eyed babies. And yet somehow the old aphorism about the cure being worse than the disease kept running in circles around in her head.

"Molly?" Joaquin prompted. "It was your idea, *no?* If you don't want to do it—"

"Yes! All right, damn it! I'll have a drink with you."

"Mm," he murmured, a smile touching his lips. "And so very politely said."

"Go soak your head," Molly muttered.

But he didn't go. He just waited patiently, watching her expectantly. For all she knew he'd stand there for the rest of the afternoon. He might still be there when Fiona and Duncan came. And she'd still be dripping in her towel.

"All right! Thank you," she bit out. And she flashed him a fierce, insincere smile because if she didn't do it, he'd probably wait for *that,* too.

"Well, it's a start," he allowed. "Next time, *querida,* combine the two—and mean it. Now, try it again."

Again? "For heaven's sakes!"

But, unfazed, he just smiled at her. Molly glared. He didn't move. Damn the man. The sun would probably set and he would still be waiting.

"Oh, all right." Molly bared her teeth in a semblance of a grin. "Thank you," she said through it. "I'd like that."

"See, I knew you could do it. And I can tell how completely thrilled you are," he drawled sarcastically and screwed up his face in such an absolutely horrible expression that Molly burst out laughing.

And at the sight he nodded. "Ah, yes. *Mucho mejor.* Much better, *querida.* Like that. You have a beautiful smile. Truly. Now say, 'Yes, thank you, Joaquin. I'd love to.'"

Molly tried to wipe the lingering smile off her face, but it wasn't quite possible. That truly had sounded sincere. Did he mean it? Did he really think her smile was beautiful? Shaking her head in confusion, Molly repeated his words—all but his name. She couldn't quite bring herself to say that.

Fortunately he didn't insist. "Bravo," he approved. "Very good. I'll pick you up at seven-thirty."

"I can meet you there."

Dark brows came down in a scowl. "No, you cannot meet me there. I am inviting you, Molly. I will escort you. This is not a negotiation. It's a date."

"But—"

"A date," he said firmly.

"It's a lesson," she corrected him.

"A learning-by-doing lesson," he retorted. "And now you say, 'That would be very nice, thank you.'"

The battle of wills began again. Molly wondered how long she could make him just stand there waiting. Probably not as long as he could make her stand here wearing only a towel.

"That would be very nice. Thank you," she grumbled, remembering to tack on a smile at the last second. And was annoyed to find she was pleased to see the swift grin of approval that replaced Joaquin's frown.

"*Bueno.* I'll see you at seven-thirty. *Hasta entonces,* Molly."

"Um...*hasta entonces,*" Molly mumbled, then stood clutching her towel, feeling a mixture of relief and panic— what *had* she got herself into?—as Joaquin gave her a wink as he went on his way.

IT WASN'T A DATE.

It was *not* a date!

No matter what he'd said, Molly knew better. Joaquin Santiago might be taking her to the Grouper, but it was nothing like the way a real date with God's gift to women would be.

So why were her palms sweating? And why was her stomach swirling? And why had she spent the last hour ransacking her closet for something attractive to wear?

It wasn't as if something was going to miraculously materialize in her closet. Since she'd quit teaching and moved back to the island she hadn't bought new clothes. She made do with Hugh's and Lachlan's cast-offs and a couple of swimsuits.

She did what she could, putting on the most respectable pair of shorts she owned—the only pair that had not been Hugh's or Lachlan's first—and a clean T-shirt without a beer or a junkanoo slogan on it. She even tucked it in.

It wasn't as if she was out to impress Mr. Hotshot Latin Lover, after all. She was going with him to learn from him, not tantalize him.

He was her "teacher," not her date.

Still, she felt a very unfamiliar unsteadiness when, at precisely seven-thirty, there came a knock on the door. Taking a quick—and she hoped, calming—breath, Molly jerked open the door.

Joaquin Santiago, in all his handsome glory, black hair flopping across his forehead, stood on her porch, shaking his head and saying mournfully, "I liked the towel better."

Molly's face flamed, but she said gruffly, "You almost got it. I only have shorts and T-shirts."

"You wore a dress for Lachlan's wedding."

"I borrowed it from Carin, and you know it."

"I thought you might have decided to buy one since you looked spectacular in it."

Molly didn't know what to say to that. She wasn't used to having a man comment on her appearance or even, in fact, *noticing* her appearance. She shrugged awkwardly. "No place to wear it."

"Maybe if you had one, Carter would think of someplace you could go."

"Carson," she corrected him sharply, and he smiled and nodded, and she narrowed her gaze at him, wondering if he'd given Carson the wrong name on purpose. It was hard to tell what Joaquin did on purpose—besides flirt and play soccer. And he wasn't doing the latter anymore. "And Carson's too busy for us to go anywhere."

"Which we will have to change." Joaquin offered her his arm. "Come along."

Molly stood stock-still and looked at him, appalled. "I can't take your arm!"

"No? *¿Por qué?* Why not?"

"Because…because…" she sputtered "…everyone would think we were going out!"

"*Sí.* We are going out."

"Not…like that!"

"Like what?"

"Like a…couple!"

"Tonight we are a couple."

"We're not! It's lessons!"

"As in teacher and student, *sí?* Then you will take my arm as a part of the lesson, *querida.*" He smiled. The arm awaited her, raised a bit.

"I don't—"

"Who is the teacher?" he asked her, his tone gently mocking.

She glared. "Carson wouldn't like it."

Totally untrue. Carson wouldn't care at all. Carson wasn't the least bit jealous. But Molly cared. Tongues would wag. Carson wouldn't care about that, either. But she did. She did not want to have to explain to anyone *why* she was seen walking arm in arm with Joaquin Santiago.

"We can walk to the Grouper together," she told him firmly. "But that's all. We're *friends.*"

Joaquin didn't look convinced. But he shrugged. "Very well. If you are afraid that your reputation will suffer."

His gallantry irritated her further. "I just don't want people talking," she explained.

"Perhaps you would like to walk five paces behind me?"

"Don't be an ass. We'll just walk together. I always walk with Carson," she said even as she edged carefully past him down the steps.

He caught up with her and reached around her before she could open the gate and did it himself, then gave her a mocking courtly bow and waved her through. "After you."

Molly slipped past, tempted to hurry on, but mastered her instinct to bolt and waited while he latched the gate again.

He smiled approvingly. "So," he said. "We walk. Without touching? Do you and Carter walk without touching?"

"Carson," she corrected through her teeth, knowing now that he was doing it on purpose. "He touches me," she said defensively.

He often slung an arm over her shoulders or gave her a bone-crushing hug or grabbed her hand and hauled her wherever he wanted her to go. But something in her tone must have conveyed a certain hesitancy because Joaquin nodded.

"We'll work on that," he said. "And the clothes," he added.

"Clothes?" Molly echoed warily.

Joaquin slanted her a grin. "It's easier to seduce most men if they don't think you're one, too."

"Very funny. But unnecessary. Carson knows I'm a woman."

"Does he?" The question was mild but cut to the bone. And apparently realizing it, Joaquin reached out and took her hand. "The thing is, *querida,* you want the awareness to hit him squarely between the eyes. Men don't understand subtlety." He had pulled her to a stop in the middle of the road and was looking earnestly into her eyes.

The look hit *her* squarely between the eyes, that was for sure. Molly wetted her lips. "I can get something," she said.

"We will go shopping."

"You can make me a list."

But he shook his head. "No. I have to tell you my reactions." He started walking again, pulling her along with him, though whether he'd forgotten he wasn't supposed to be holding her hand or whether he intended to keep a grip on her so she wouldn't run away, she didn't know.

"Shopping where?" Molly said warily.

"Wherever you want. The boutique at the Mirabelle. Erica's in town."

Syd bought her clothes at Erica's. It had lovely expensive stuff. The boutique was even pricier. Molly almost never set foot in either of them. "I don't shop there."

"You don't shop."

She lifted a defiant chin and jerked her hand out of his. "I haven't needed to. I can. I will," she vowed.

"And I'll come with you."

"Not to Erica's!"

"Why not?"

"Because people would talk!"

He rolled his eyes. "So we'll go to another island. We'll go to Nassau. Or Miami."

"Miami?"

"Why not? Surely they won't talk in Miami."

"No, but—"

"Stop arguing, *querida,*" he said and reached out and snagged her hand, this time lacing his fingers firmly through hers.

She jerked to a stop. "What are you doing?"

"Little things. Connecting things." He met her gaze with a heavy-lidded one of his own. My God, he had beautiful eyes.

Molly swallowed. "Why?" she demanded and hated that her voice sounded shaky.

"So you can do them with Carter."

"Carson!"

He shrugged. His eyes never left hers. They were mesmerizing. Molly tried to remember if Carson had ever linked his fingers with hers. She couldn't. She tried to remember if she had ever tried it with him. She couldn't.

But Joaquin was right—it certainly emphasized the connection!

"Right," she said. "Got it." She tried to unlace her fingers, but he didn't let go. They were stopped in the middle of the street, staring into each other's eyes as his thumb slid lightly over her fingers making them tingle.

How did he *do* that?

It made her so aware of him. She dropped her gaze—and found herself looking at his mouth. Would he kiss her? Molly ran her tongue over her lips.

Suddenly her hand was dropped. Joaquin stepped back, jamming his into his pockets and clearing his throat. "So," he said brusquely. "You've got the point then, *sí?* Very well. Come on. Let's go."

THE WOMAN WAS A MENACE.

Molly McGillivray's big green eyes could make a man forget his best intentions right in the middle of a public road!

He was crazy to be doing this. Insane. He should have told her it was a stupid stupid stupid idea—this business of "seduction lessons." He should have his head examined for agreeing. In fact he'd turned up on her doorstep this afternoon to do exactly that.

It had been boredom that had made him say yes. And his perennial need to take on a hopeless challenge. And perhaps, he admitted, the memory of her at Lachlan's wedding. But sanity had prevailed when she'd left.

He was no Henry Higgins. And she was sure as hell no Eliza Doolittle! And there were some things even he couldn't manage. He'd gone to her house to tell her so.

And then she'd come downstairs in that towel.

All thoughts of telling her no went right out of his head.

Every time he shut his eyes, he could still see her as she'd been when she'd come down the stairs, lots of bare creamy skin with a bright yellow towel tucked just above her breasts and stopping well above her knees. Used to seeing Molly

McGillivray in her brothers' hand-me-downs, the sight of her on the hoof, so to speak, had very nearly welded his tongue to the roof of his mouth. It had certainly scrambled his brain.

He'd been mesmerized. Tantalized. Maybe, he'd thought, there was more Eliza Doolittle in her than he'd thought. Heaven knew there was certainly some raw material to work with.

But raw was definitely what it was.

Molly didn't have a clue how enticing she was. She had no idea of her own ability to arouse a man. That little thing she'd done with her tongue, licking her lips when they were standing there just now was a case in point.

His whole body had gone on alert. In fact it responded so quickly and vehemently he'd taken a quick step back.

Of course Molly—*gracias a Dios*—hadn't noticed.

But he'd have to watch his step. He was supposed to be teaching her how to be seductive, not allowing himself to be seduced by her.

Seduced by Molly McGillivray?

The thought wasn't as bizarre as he might have wished. Another time—and another woman—he wouldn't mind a little fooling around. But she was his best friend's sister. Therefore she was like his own sister.

But he wasn't thinking about her as his sister as he hurried to catch up with her. She was already inside the Grouper and about to sit at the bar when he grabbed her hand again.

"It is customary," he told her, "not to share one's date with everyone at the bar."

"What?" Molly looked at him blankly, waggling her fingers at the bartender in greeting.

Joaquin turned her so she faced him. "A couple," he instructed her, "must focus on each other."

"But—"

He wasn't listening. With her wrist manacled by his fingers, he towed her to a table in the back of the room. "Here. We will sit here."

"But the music—"

"Is not the issue. The issue is to get to know each other." He let go long enough to pull out a chair for her. "Sit."

She gave him a mutinous look. "Carson and I already know each other," she said. "And I like being where I can hear."

"You can hear if you stay home," Joaquin said which was only the truth. "Sit."

He thought she might argue further, but finally, reluctantly, she sat. He had barely sat down opposite her, when she bounced to her feet again.

"Where are you going?"

"To get the beer. I think a pitcher—"

He caught her hand. "No."

"You don't want a beer?" She looked perplexed.

"Beer is fine. I'll get it. You're not waiting tables here. You're on a date."

She shifted restlessly. The skin of her wrist was soft under his fingers. He lifted her fingers and brushed his lips across them. She jerked but he held her fast.

"Sit down, *querida*," he murmured. "Just sit. Enjoy. Don't clean the tables. Don't go visit your friends. Wait for me."

Because, damn it, he *wanted* her to wait for him. He wanted to be the focus of her attention.

She looked doubtful, but finally gave a small jerky nod and sat down again dutifully, folded her hands, then gave him a beatific smile. It was such a sweet smile—so unlike Molly— that he gave her a narrow look, wondering what he'd forgotten to forbid her to do.

"Wait," he said again. "I'll be right back." Then, giving her one last nail-her-to-the-chair look, he hurried to the bar. Another night he would have stopped to chat, to flirt, to tease, to charm the women in his way. Tonight he was on a mission. So he smiled and sidestepped them all, ignored Michael the bartender's curious look, and returned with a pitcher and two glasses of beer in a matter of minutes.

Molly, he was relieved to note, was still there.

He poured the beer and pushed a glass across the table for her. She wrapped her hand around it and said politely, "Thank you."

"My pleasure." He sat down opposite her and focused on her. "Now," he said, "we talk."

"About what?" She licked her lips again.

His gaze went straight to her mouth. He swallowed. "We get to know each other."

"But we already do, Carson and I. I told you that."

Forget Carson, he wanted to say. But he was the reason they were here, of course. So Joaquin raked his fingers through his hair and said, "There must be things about him that you don't know. What makes him tick? What drives him? What matters most?" He was talking off the top of his head, just wallowing in the green magic of her eyes. "Do you know all that?"

"I—maybe not," she admitted. "Or I wouldn't be doing this, would I?"

"Exactly. So you focus. You pay attention to him. You ask questions. Yes?"

"Okay, yes." She sipped her beer and did that quick tongue thing to her lips again.

Joaquin felt his blood run hot and did his best to distract himself. "So you try, all right?"

She touched her upper lip with her tongue. "You mean, ask about what he—you—most care about?"

"Yes." *And stop doing that thing with your tongue!*

"All right." Molly nodded, pressed her lips together and looked down into her glass a long moment, then she lifted her gaze and met his. "Are you afraid to come watch Lachlan and the kids play soccer?"

"What?" He stared at her, gut punched.

"You don't come. I know he's asked you. But you never come."

His jaw clenched. "I don't talk about soccer," he said harshly.

She looked genuinely surprised. "Why not?"

"Because—" He hesitated. He didn't want to continue. Didn't want to go there. But there didn't seem to be any way out. The noise and commotion in the bar swirled around them, but he didn't hear any of it. He heard the roar of blood in his head and the echo of Molly's frank question.

"Wrong question?" she asked gently when he didn't reply at once.

His fingers tightened on the glass he held. He let out the breath that seemed to be choking him. "No," he said honestly. "I asked for it." Because he had. He'd challenged her—and she'd challenged him right back.

"I don't talk about it because it makes people uncomfortable. It makes *me* uncomfortable." He swallowed. "It hurts."

He expected some platitude, a you-don't-know-how-lucky-you-are comment like many he'd heard when people learned he'd recovered from the paralysis with no real lingering physical damage.

But Molly didn't say that. She didn't say anything for a moment. Then she nodded. "It must," she said. "I can't imagine, having your life snatched away in an instant."

That was it, exactly.

"I saw what Lachlan went through when he quit. He needed to find his place, find out what he was without soccer being the focus. But it was his choice when he left. The way it happened to you—" she lifted her eyes and met his gaze sympathetically "—it must be like losing a part of yourself, like losing a limb."

"My heart."

He had never said that aloud. Had never admitted to anyone how deep the loss had cut. He'd been stoic, determined. First to recover, to play again. Then to cope resolutely when he could not. His whole demeanor had been unstintingly positive. Relentlessly upbeat.

Of course he was lucky. He knew that. He even said it when everyone else did. And he would be fine, he assured them all. And he'd bottled all the pain and disorientation up. It seemed insignificant compared to other peoples' problems. It *was* insignificant. He knew that.

He had so much to be grateful for that it seemed churlish to complain about the one thing he couldn't do. So he never had.

He still didn't complain, but because Molly sat there, sipping her beer, focusing on him, listening to him, encouraging him by her silence, he talked.

Slowly, wryly almost, he talked about what soccer had meant to him from the time he'd been a little boy. How it had been a way of being himself and not just a part of the Santiago corporate empire. Playing soccer was to do something that no other Santiago did. His father had rarely even come to see him play.

Molly had been surprised at that, and indignant on his behalf. But Joaquin had shaken his head. "It didn't matter to me," he said. "I didn't do it for him. I did it for myself. Soccer was *mine*. It was where I belonged. Where I grew up. Where I learned what mattered."

He talked about how he loved the blend of teamwork and individual skill, of talent and sheer hard work, of a hundred things he hadn't even realized he thought or felt. About the challenge and the glory and how you didn't get one without the other. About how it called forth reserves he didn't even know he had.

He started slowly, but as he talked, it was as if the trickle became a flood, and once begun, he couldn't stop.

Molly didn't try to stop him. On the contrary, she nodded, listening intently, rarely speaking except to ask a question or make a perceptive comment.

So he was stunned when, not long after, she said, "I guess we'd better let Michael lock up."

"What?" He looked around to see that almost everyone had cleared out and the bartender was wiping down the bar. Disbelieving, he stared at his watch. It was nearly one. "I talked the whole night?'' He was mortified. ''Why didn't you tell me to shut up?''

Molly laughed. ''Because I didn't want you to. Easier for me to listen.''

He grimaced, aware of how much he had told her that he'd never told anyone else. The woman was a sorceress, he thought irritably. ''I was supposed to be teaching you,'' he said gruffly.

''You did.''

''Yeah, right.''

''You gave me some confidence. It's nice to know that a superhero can bleed like everyone else.''

He stared at her. ''What?''

She winced and her face flushed. ''Sorry. Lack of tact strikes again. I just meant, you're always so capable. So in control. Nothing every bothers you. It was…I don't know…comforting, I suppose…to discover you're human, too.''

''I'm glad you're happy now,'' he said crossly.

''Don't.''

He frowned. ''Don't what?''

''Don't spoil it.'' She gave him a smile—a genuine, heart-felt Molly McGillivray smile that did odd things to his insides. ''It was very nice. Really. I don't mean your pain was nice. But that you…shared it.'' She shrugged awkwardly. ''I had a good time.''

''Listening to me spill my guts.'' He still didn't like it. He hated feeling exposed, but it was his own fault. ''Come on,'' he said gruffly. ''I'll walk you home.''

''You don't—'' she began, then stopped and smiled. ''All right.''

An agreeable Molly McGillivray was more unnerving than a contrary one. Especially when she waited politely for him and rested her hand on his arm as they went out the door.

''I thought we weren't touching,'' he said.

''That was then,'' she said breezily and patted his arm.

Definitely unnerving. But he went along with it, steered her out the door and down the steps and onto the pavement where he expected she would pull back. But she didn't.

Everything he'd told her earlier about touch and connections was absolutely true. And the feel of her fingers on his arm made him increasingly aware of it.

"How am I doing?" she asked.

"What?" He dragged his mind back to the purpose of the exercise. "Fine." He cleared his throat. "You're doing fine."

Too damn good as a matter of fact. First she got him to spill his guts. Now she was turning him on with the merest touch of her fingers.

"There's almost a full moon out tonight," she said.

"I didn't notice," he said, walking a bit faster, wanting to get her home.

"I would think that would be something I should take advantage of."

"Don't get ahead of yourself," he said sharply.

She stopped. "What do you mean?" she looked at him wide-eyed and guileless, and he could see her very clearly in the moonlight she'd just mentioned.

"I mean you need to take it slowly. One step at a time."

"But you said I was doing fine."

"Who's teaching whom?" he snapped.

She looked chagrined. "You're saying I'm being too forward?"

"No! Yes! I—" He raked a hand through his hair. "I just think you need to, um, pace yourself. Let Carter take the lead."

"*Carson* doesn't seem to want to take the lead," she reminded him. "If he did, we wouldn't be doing this."

"Right," he said distractedly. "But it's late. And you've done enough for one night." He started to take her hand and head up the hill, then thought better of it and jammed his into his pockets. But he did start walking, and was relieved when she hurried to catch up with him.

Neither spoke the rest of the way up the hill to her house. He opened the gate and held it for her to go through, which she did. But instead of going straight on up to her door, she stopped.

"Should I invite you in?"

"No!" He swallowed and moderated his tone. "Not on a first date," he explained.

"But it wouldn't be my first date with Carson."

"Doesn't matter," he said firmly. "Go on in now." Before he changed his mind and took her up on it. "Good night."

Molly smiled at him. *"Buenas noches,* Joaquin. *Gracias."*

Her soft Spanish sent a curl of desire right through him. *"Buenas noches,* Molly," he said gruffly. "Now go inside."

She started to move away, then stopped. "What about good-night kisses?"

He felt a strangling sensation in his throat. "Molly!"

"I know, I know. I'm rushing things. It's too soon. I'm too pushy."

She said it all for him, so he didn't have to answer, which was good because he didn't have the words and he would have been happy to kiss her senseless. Instead he silently pointed toward her door.

Molly grinned, then reached out and touched his hand fleetingly. "Thanks." Then she turned and hurried away. He breathed easier as he shut the gate.

But on the porch she stopped and looked back. "Joaquin?"

"What?" He kept his voice carefully neutral.

"When do I get my next lesson?"

"We'll see."

"I need—"

"We'll see, Molly!"

He had to recover from this one first.

CHAPTER THREE

IT WAS A BIT LIKE walking on a tightrope, this seduction business.

Exhilarating. Heady. Awesome.

A little bit scary when you got right down to it. The sizzle, the spark, the almost electric connection she'd felt every time she'd stared into Joaquin Santiago's eyes last night was like nothing Molly had ever felt before.

She'd practically been caroming off the walls when she'd got home. Her brain had been buzzing with all the things he'd told her—about himself, about his life, his family, his feelings about soccer—all of it so totally unexpected, so completely *not* the sort of inane boy-meets-girl small talk she'd expected he would drill her in, that she couldn't sleep.

She tried. But she tossed and turned and muttered and rolled. She tangled herself in the sheet and twisted so much that once she almost fell out onto the floor. Finally she got up and made herself some of Auntie Esme's sleep potion which, with its reliance upon a generous dollop of rum, on top of the beer she'd drunk at the Grouper, finally did the trick.

So she slept. But even in sleep, her brain was busy creating the most incredible dreams. Vivid dreams. Sensual dreams. Erotic dreams.

Molly couldn't remember ever having had an erotic dream in her life. But she did now—and all of them were about Joaquin Santiago!

Last night she'd been eager for more lessons. Today she

realized that it was a very good thing Hugh had deputized her to fly a bunch of tourists to Nassau for the whole day while he was in Miami.

It would give her a little breathing room, some time and distance to regain her equilibrium and sort out the dreams—and the feelings—Joaquin had evoked last night.

They were, she reminded herself as she gobbled down her breakfast and ran a comb through her hair, nothing more than the feelings she'd been hoping for. Feelings of awareness of herself as a woman, of sexual attraction for a man, of the desire to flirt with him, the urge to entice him. And more.

In fact they were exactly what she'd been looking for.

Of course they were about the completely wrong man!

But—and it was important to keep this firmly in mind—at least the feelings existed.

Deep down in a place Molly didn't even want to acknowledge, she'd begun to be afraid they might not. Ever since her brothers had courted and married their wives, Molly had begun to realize that what existed so far between Carson and herself was nowhere near as intense as what existed between Lachlan and Fiona and Hugh and Sydney. Recently, though, she'd begun to worry that the problem wasn't her lack of feminine wiles, but, in a word, frigidity.

After last night she was no longer worried about that!

She grinned now, feeling lighter and still more exhilarated than she had in weeks. Maybe she would go shopping for a dress while she was waiting. She'd feel better about doing it there where local eyes wouldn't be speculating on just exactly what tomboy Molly was up to.

Maybe she would wear it for her next "lesson." Grinning, Molly hurried down the hill toward the dock where a group of tourists already gathered waiting for her by the launch that would take them out to the sea plane for their journey to Nassau and a day spent doing the galleries and museums learning about the cultural blend in Bahamian art.

"Hope I'm not late," she said to Sophy, the tour leader.

"You're right on time," Sophy said. "We just got here, too. We picked up a last-minute participant who needed to get to Nassau. I hope that's not a problem."

"Of course not. Always room for one more," Molly said, beaming at the group. They were mostly middle-aged, mostly well heeled, mostly European travelers in search of a little art, a little culture and a not-too-far-off-the-beaten-path holiday, with a bit of shopping thrown in.

"*Gracias,*" a smooth familiar masculine voice said, and the group parted enough so that she found herself staring into Joaquin Santiago's deep-brown eyes.

Completely unbidden, Molly's heart kicked over in her chest, her brain was seized by a kaleidoscope of all the fantasies she'd entertained last night, and she was sure her cheeks had gone scarlet.

"You! What are you—" she sputtered.

"I believe we talked about more lessons?" He was smiling at her.

"Not now!" Molly was horrified.

"Lessons?" Sophy's hearing was, sadly, excellent, her expression bright and inquisitive as she looked from one to the other of them. "What sort of lessons?"

"Flying lessons," Molly said quickly before Joaquin could even open his mouth. "He's interested in taking flying lessons. We were discussing it last night," she said, lying through her teeth.

"Is that what you were talking about? I noticed you two huddling together at a table in the back at the Grouper," Sophy said. "You looked very...intense."

"It's a big commitment," Molly said. Then she turned to Joaquin. "But today is probably not a good day. I'm going to be gone all day." She gave him a speaking look, one which she hoped he understood meant *go away.*

"Oh, I'm sure I can learn a lot just watching you." He gave her one of his most dazzling smiles, his own expression daring her to challenge him.

Molly didn't take the dare. Not in front of Sophy and half a dozen interested bystanders. "Suit yourself," she said gruffly. "But I'm going to be very busy."

"Not all day, surely," he countered, then grinned. It was one of those flirting grins he bestowed on women he met in bars. She'd seen him do it a hundred times or more.

Was this the lesson, then?

She felt disoriented and confused and last night's heady power was fast evaporating. Because she could think of nothing useful to say, she shook her head and turned away, trying to get her mind on her work and *off* Joaquin Santiago.

"Come along," she said to the rest of the group. "Let's get in the launch." She and Hoby the boatman helped everyone in. Molly made sure she stayed as far from Joaquin as possible. She didn't need him distracting her, and she didn't need him giving Sophy any information for the island telegraph. So she concentrated on talking to a couple from Oxford, all the while wishing she weren't so aware of every move Joaquin made.

When they reached the plane, she scrambled in and left Sophy to figure out where everyone was going to sit. It was something she normally did herself as it was a good way to chat with the guests and make them feel at home. But today she didn't feel at home herself. So she settled in the pilot's seat and made herself concentrate on the preflight checks. That way she could remain aloof from the group and not have to watch the scramble among the women in the group to see who would get to sit next to Joaquin.

It was a bit disconcerting moments later to look around and find him climbing in to sit next to her.

"What are you doing? You can't sit up here!"

"Of course I can. I have to," he added piously. "How can I learn to fly if I don't?" He was laughing at her and she knew it.

She scowled furiously. "Don't be ridiculous."

He shrugged. "I'm not the one who told Sophy I was taking flying lessons. She said I must sit where I could see what you were doing."

Molly gave him a narrow, steely look. But he just smiled and shrugged again. "It was very kind of her."

"Oh, yes, very," Molly retorted drily. "This is not funny. This is my job."

"And of course I will let you do it. I will be happy to watch you do it, *querida*. Maybe I will let you teach me to fly."

There was something in his tone, a soft seductive note that sent a shiver right through her.

"Stop that!" she commanded. "I have to think. I have to focus."

He folded his hands in his lap. "I will be as silent as a monk," he promised.

Yeah, right. As if that would make her less aware of him sitting just inches from her. She could see his khaki-clad thigh without even glancing out of the corner of her eye. When she moved her arm, her elbow brushed his sleeve.

"Tight quarters," he murmured.

Molly didn't answer. *Focus*, she commanded herself. *Concentrate. Pretend it's Carson sitting next to you.*

That worked. She felt calmer. Steadier. And more than a little guilty on account of it. But at least within moments she had the plane skimming across the water and lifting up into the soft-hued morning sky.

Beside her, Joaquin moved at last and sucked in his breath as he watched the island fall away behind them. "It's the most beautiful place on earth," he said softly.

She looked at him, surprised at the sentiment that so echoed her own. "It is, isn't it?"

To Molly there was nothing more gorgeous than the panorama of sky and sea and islands she enjoyed every time she took off from Pelican Cay. The last time she'd flown Carson back to Nassau, he'd spent the entire trip engrossed in paperwork. Of course he'd seen the view a hundred times or more, but so had Molly—and she could never get enough of it.

Now her gaze met Joaquin's, and she felt a quickening awareness when he smiled back at her.

Wrong man! Wrong man! Her brain cells screamed.

He was. Of course he was. She knew that. Determinedly she turned away and concentrated on flying the plane.

When they landed, a local launch picked them up from the sea plane and took them to the dock where Sophy always arranged for a van to meet them.

While every trip was slightly different, in general she would give them a quick historical tour of the island, then take them to a museum, then to lunch with an artist, and afterward to a gallery or two to meet local artists and artisans. The tour always ended at the straw market where Molly would meet them, and together they would head back to the plane.

This gave Molly the whole day free. Sometimes she spent it on the beach. Sometimes she brought a book and read. Sometimes she had a list of errands from Hugh that kept her busy, and she never minded that. But she was glad she didn't have any today. It would give her time to go to the beach for a while, then stop by a couple of the shops near the straw market and pick up a colorful dress.

But when the van reached the center of town and Sophy asked, as she always did, if Molly wanted to come along with them, she didn't say anything about her plans. She just said no thanks, she was going to be busy.

"She's coming with me," Joaquin said. And leaving Sophy with her mouth in an *O* of astonishment, he opened the door and climbed out, hauling Molly along with him.

"What are you—"

But he just steered her onto the pavement. "We'll see you at the straw market at four," he said to Sophy and waved as they disappeared into traffic. Then he turned to Molly and rubbed his hands together. "All right, then. Lesson two."

"Not funny," Molly said. "I can't believe you did that! What's Sophy going to think?"

"That you're giving me flying lessons?" He grinned.

She ground her teeth at him.

"Or—" he shrugged "—maybe that I want to spend time with you?"

"God forbid!" Molly snorted in disbelief. "If she believes that, I've got some swamp land to sell her. Besides, she knows I'm engaged to Carson."

"Then she won't think a thing of it." He grabbed her hand. "Come along. We have work to do."

"Work? What work?" Molly demanded as he hauled her along the crowded pavement. "I have plans today!"

"Oh, yes? What plans?"

She felt suddenly awkward about telling him, about having him laugh at the thought of her going shopping. "Just…plans," she muttered.

"Well, perhaps we can fit them in," he said. "But first, our lesson." He was scanning the shops along the street as if he were looking for something in particular.

"What's the lesson?" Molly demanded. "Where are we going?"

"There." He smiled as he spotted what he was looking for. "And we are going to make the most of you."

And taking her by the arm, he whisked her straight into a posh styling salon just off Bay Street. "We'll start with a haircut."

"I just got my hair cut!"

He looked down his nose at her. "By who? Hugh?"

Molly colored fiercely at the accuracy of his guess. "As a matter of fact, yes." She lifted her chin and dared him to make something of it.

He did. "As a hairstylist, Hugh's a great pilot."

"He cut hair in the Air Force." And he only ever trimmed the ends of hers. It was all she would allow.

"In the Air Force? Now there's a recommendation," Joaquin said drily. "I'm talking about a real haircut. If you're going to seduce this reluctant fiancé of yours," Joaquin persisted, "Little Orphan Annie has got to go." He gave her a gentle push further into the high-ceilinged room.

Molly glowered and muttered under her breath as she stood there, contemplating the acres of chrome and glass, the wall of gleaming mirrors and the kaleidoscope of rainbow colors splashed across the ceiling. It was so high that the palm trees artfully situated here and there didn't even have to bend their heads.

"Not exactly Hugh's front porch and the kitchen shears," she mumbled.

"Amen to that."

"Look, I appreciate the idea, but I just don't think…" she began but her voice died away as a tall elegant black woman approached, beaming. Her elaborately beaded corn rows clinked and clicked as she swayed toward them.

"Ah, good morning. How can I help you?" the woman asked in a beautifully melodious Bahamian accent.

"The lady wants a haircut," Joaquin said firmly. "And a style. Something that will bring out her best features."

Molly gave the woman full credit for not laughing. Also for not screaming for immediate emergency help. Instead she murmured, "Mmm, yes. Let me see." And keeping a carefully intent expression on her face, she glided around Molly, studying her from every vantage point.

Molly felt like a cow at the county fair. And not a prize-winning one, either. She wanted to kill Joaquin, but didn't want to get blood on the highly polished granite. Still if looks could kill bloodlessly, he'd have been lifeless on the floor.

Finally the circumnavigation ended and the woman stopped in front of her, studied her face as intently as she'd studied everything else, then reached out a beautifully manicured hand to tip Molly's chin up slightly. Then she nodded. And smiled.

"Yes," she said with considerable satisfaction. "I can do that."

She nodded confidently at Joaquin. Then she turned her gaze on Molly, her dark eyes smiling. "You are beautiful. Melisande will show the world it is so."

"I doubt it," Molly said frankly.

Melisande's brows lifted, perfect arcs of disbelief. "You doubt? Come. I will show you."

And before she knew it, Molly found herself seated in one of the styling chairs, her shoulders draped with a pristine white towel. In the mirror she could see Joaquin standing there watching, grinning.

Then she was spun around and tipped back so her head hung over the sink and a spray of water, temperature controlled no doubt, cascaded over her skull.

Strong but gentle hands worked up a lather. Washed. Rinsed. Then repeated the process. It was heavenly. And Molly was, after the first few moments, powerless to resist.

She floated on the sensations. Only when Melisande finished and wrapped her hair in a towel and tipped her upright again did Molly come back to reality and realize that the whole time Joaquin had been standing there watching her.

She stuck her tongue out at him.

SEDUCTION WAS NOT unlike soccer.

It was fun. It was exhilarating. And played at the highest level with a worthy opponent, it was unpredictable. The outcome was always tantalizing—and always uncertain.

Since he'd come to Pelican Cay, his nightly flirtations had been so predictable that Joaquin had found them almost boring. Like playing against amateurs, flirting with women who were predisposed to fall into bed with him was a pleasant diversion, but hardly a challenge. It passed the time. But it never engaged his interest except on a physical level—and then only briefly.

The outcome, of course, was never in question.

It was totally different dealing with Molly McGillivray.

Molly was a challenge and a half. She was as stubborn as her brothers, as tough as old boots and as unaware of her own appeal as an innocent child. There was no artifice, no affectation about her. She had asked him to teach her how to seduce—but if last night's encounter was anything to go by, she had nothing to learn. She was a natural.

He'd been demanding that she "pay attention" to him, expecting merely that she would meet his gaze so that he could teach her a little about flirtatious eye contact, about the casual inadvertent touch—and she had paid far closer attention than that.

She had gone right for his heart. She had focused on the one thing that mattered, had asked him with complete sincerity about the one thing that no one had dared ask him about. And there had been such gentle concern in her question that he'd felt compelled to answer her.

She'd off-balanced him, caught him unawares. And so he'd talked. And talked. Made a fool of himself, he'd thought after, annoyed at how much of himself he'd revealed—and at how little he knew about her.

He'd known Molly McGillivray for years. But now he could see that he didn't really know her at all.

She had been one surprise after another—starting with the eyeful he'd got when she'd come downstairs in that towel and ending with the not-in-the-least-diminished desire to find out what was under that towel. He'd gone back to the Moonstone wondering what her lips would taste like, how her body would feel pressed against his, what it would be like to make love to her.

And then, of course, there was the knowledge that he wasn't going to find out.

She had a fiancé. That was the point of the whole "lessons" business, wasn't it? Bringing the reluctant Carson Sawyer up to snuff.

Yes. It was.

And yet—

Joaquin jammed his hands into his pockets and rocked back and forth on the balls of his feet, balancing, considering. And he didn't think the outcome should be that predictable.

Maybe it was the competitor in him, but it seemed to him that if Carson Sawyer really loved Molly, if he was worthy of her love, he would do more than simply notice her, more than lie back and agree to be seduced by her.

He would fight for her.

He would move heaven and earth for her.

He would— Dear God.

His thoughts stopped dead as the stylist stepped aside and right there in the mirror Joaquin found himself staring at the most stunningly beautiful woman he'd ever seen in his life.

Molly's riot of coppery curls was gone. In its place was a short sleek shiny cap of auburn hair. It was almost boyish— and in being so, revealed that the woman who wore it was not boyish at all. No boy could possibly have that slender neck, those delicate features, that gamine look and those curving lips.

What the stylist, Melisande, had done with a pair of scissors on Molly McGillivray's hair was the sort of thing Leonardo da Vinci had done with a chisel and slab of granite. She'd found the beauty in Molly and released it. She'd cut off a mound of wild curling hair and turned Little Orphan Annie into a delicate, fine-boned, absolutely stunning woman.

Joaquin's breath caught in his chest. He stared, poleaxed.

And so did Molly. First at her own reflection, then at him. Their eyes met in the mirror and locked.

She looked stunned and, he thought, almost frightened. As if she didn't know how to handle the woman she was discovering inside her skin.

He'd be only too happy to show her. The thought made him smile, made him breathe again. He smiled at her and felt a stab of desire when she gave him a nervous, tentative smile in return.

Then Melisande broke the moment as she set down the scissors and turned Molly's chair, breaking their gaze. Ruffling her fingers through Molly's hair, she played with the short locks, tousling them, regarding her handiwork critically. Then she stepped back and nodded her satisfaction.

"So," she said to Molly with a smile, "now do you believe me?"

And Molly ran her tongue over her lips, then nodded jerkily. "It's, um, pretty amazing," she allowed.

Melisande laughed. "I know you like." She was satisfied with that. Then she turned to him. "And you? What do you think? It suits her, yes?"

"Oh, yes." His voice was husky with desire, and he knew Melisande understood the reason even if Molly was totally unaware.

Melisande laughed softly, pleased. Then back to business, she reached down and picked up one of Molly's hands. "Next we must do something about these."

Instantly Molly snatched her hand back and shook her head. "No! It's pointless. I work—"

But before he could stop himself, Joaquin cut in, "Yes."

Molly's eyes darted to the mirror to meet his. "They're not *your* hands!"

He didn't care. For once he wanted them as soft as the tender flesh of her arm that he'd felt under his fingers last night. He didn't stop to think about why. "Not my hands," he agreed loftily. "But I am the teacher."

"Carson won't notice—"

"I will," Joaquin said. He already had. And for reasons he refused to consider more closely he wanted her hands as soft as the rest of her.

Molly glared. He met her gaze implacably. Melisande looked from one to the other.

Joaquin folded his arms across his chest. "It is for your own good," he told Molly.

She looked mutinous. Her fingers balled into fists. But then, slowly, she released them, splayed them, looked down at them and sighed.

"All right," she said at last and stuck out her hands to Melisande. "Do with me what you will."

AS SHE GOT HER HANDS manicured—and how insane was that for a mechanic, for goodness' sake?—Molly kept sneaking glances in the mirror, startled every time she glimpsed the redheaded woman in the manicurist's chair who met her gaze.

She'd been horrified when Melisande had begun chopping off her hair. For years Molly thought her mop of curls was the only way people could tell she was a girl. The short boyish haircut the stylist had given her should have made her look as tomboyish as she was.

Instead it made her look almost delicate. Delicate? Molly nearly snorted. But then she recalled that it had certainly made Joaquin do a double-take. When he'd met her gaze in the mirror, he'd looked almost stunned.

No more stunned than she was. She glanced in the mirror again, intrigued by this stranger looking back at her with a hint of a secret smile on her face. It was like finding out she had secrets even *she* didn't know she had.

So, the haircut was terrific. She had to give Joaquin credit for that.

But the manicure? It was insane. It was a complete waste of time. And money. It probably wouldn't even work. Certainly the manicurist had gulped when she'd taken a look at Molly's callused, oil-stained hands. But then she'd smiled gamely, as if she'd been asked to climb the manicurist's Everest—and set to work.

Now as the woman smoothed the sweet-smelling lotion into her hands, Molly felt ticklish and just a little vulnerable. And surprisingly pleased. All her nerve ends tingled and she sighed with pleasure. Her resistance waned.

She leaned back in the chair and closed her eyes.

"Enjoy," the manicurist murmured.

And oddly, Molly did. She imagined what it would be like to have hands like this all the time—hands so sensitive that they would revel in stroking the roughness of a whiskered jaw and the silky softness of thick black hair.

Brown hair, she corrected herself, eyes snapping open. Carson had *brown* hair!

It was the man prowling out in the waiting area whose hair was as black as night. It was that man's hair she had touched in last night's dream. Instinctively her fingers clenched.

"No!" The manicurist flattened them again. "Relax," she said softly, massaging Molly's fingers. "Just relax now and close your eyes."

But Molly wasn't about to do that. She sat rigid, eyes wide open for the rest of the manicure, afraid to daydream again.

"Let's see," Joaquin said when she came back to the waiting area. He held out his hands imperiously. When she didn't immediately respond, he reached for her hands and took them possessively in his own.

"It's no big deal," Molly muttered even as he admired them, ran his thumbs over them, making her shiver with awareness. "I don't know why I bothered," she grumbled, wishing he'd let go. "They'll be horrible in twelve hours time."

"But now they are exquisite," he said, and he lifted one and pressed his lips against it.

"Joaquin!" She jerked her hand to get away. But he held it fast, rubbed his lips against it, all the while watching her for a reaction. "Stop that!"

He lifted his lips long enough to smile devilishly at her. "No." And damned if he didn't kiss the other one as well.

Molly felt her insides tighten. She held herself stiff and resisting. Then a strand of black hair brushed against the back of her hand and she jumped.

"What is it? What's wrong?"

"N-nothing." She yanked her hands out of his and twisted them together behind her back, ignoring the tsking sound of the manicurist who clearly disapproved. "I just—I just think it was a waste," Molly muttered.

"No," he disagreed. "It is good. They are soft. Just like the rest of you."

"As if you'd know." She glared at him, embarrassed.

"I would like to know," he said softly making her blood run hot.

"Stop it!"

He smiled guilelessly. "You asked for it."

"Yes, but not…not…" Not to feel like this! Not to be so aware of him. Not to still be able to feel the tingle of the touch of his lips against the backs of her hands even when his lips were nowhere near them.

She didn't want to feel this way! Not about him! It was Carson she needed to think about. Not bloody black-haired Joaquin Santiago!

Cool it, she told herself. Just calm down.

He was flirting with her. He didn't mean anything by it. He was *teaching* her, for heaven's sake. It was her own foolishness—her own heightened awareness—that was making it out to be more than it was.

"You're such a girl," Hugh had always said disparagingly when they were growing up and she would let her flyaway emotions get the best of her instead of being logical and sensible like him.

Don't be such a girl, she told herself sharply. And deliberately, coolly she turned away from Joaquin to pay the cashier and get herself under control. By the time she was putting her wallet away, she was feeling better. Calmer. More businesslike. It had cost an arm and a leg to look this beautiful. As long as she was paying for it she felt more in control.

And even if she blew the seduction thing, she didn't doubt that Carson would notice the haircut. *Carson,* she said over again in her mind. *Carson. Carson. Carson.* It helped to think his name. It was easier to visualize him—his quirky grin, his twice-broken nose, his light-blue eyes that crinkled when he grinned. His *brown* sun-streaked hair. As she catalogued his features in her mind she felt calmer, cooler, more collected.

"Ready?" A smooth baritone jerked her back to reality.

Molly wiped her hands down the sides of her shorts. "Yes," she said as he opened the door and she stepped out into the heat of the midmorning Bahamian sun. Then, stopping on the pavement, she turned to smile up at him.

"Well," she said brightly, "that was a first. I never would have done that without you, believe me. So thank you for the lesson."

He inclined his head. "*De nada.* You are welcome." Then he held out his arm to her.

She stared. "What? I don't want to keep you. I'm sure you have other things to do today."

"I do," he agreed. "So come along. We're going shopping."

"But I—"

They went shopping.

It wasn't exactly like being Cinderella with her own fairy godmother and a couple of mice waving magic wands and conjuring up gorgeous clothes, decking her out in finery and transforming her into a princess.

On the contrary, it was exactly like being dragged through half a dozen Nassau boutiques by a cross between Henry Higgins and the Spanish Inquisition intent on outfitting her from top to toes.

Dresses and trousers, tops and bottoms appeared and disappeared briskly as Joaquin studied them, then her, then decreed which ones she should try on. Molly couldn't imagine either of her brothers going anywhere near a boutique and feeling comfortable about it, but Joaquin seemed perfectly at home.

He would, she thought. He had probably outfitted a dozen mistresses this way. The thought was surprisingly annoying and made her scowl fiercely.

"Don't make faces," he said sharply. "Turn around. Let me see that from the back."

"There isn't any back," Molly said tartly. It was a sundress cut low with criss-cross straps. It was flirty and feminine and it didn't have pockets. Where would she put her hands?

"Very nice," he purred. "Put that aside," he said to the saleslady.

"I didn't say I wanted it," Molly protested.

"But you look beautiful in it," the saleslady assured her. "And you want to look beautiful for your man, don't you?"

"He's *not* my man!" Molly said, embarrassed.

"I'm her teacher," Joaquin agreed equably, making her want to throttle him. But he only smiled blandly when she ground her teeth. "Try this." He plucked a severe plain green silk dress off a hanger and thrust it at her.

"That? It looks like an emerald-green crayon wrapper," she argued.

Wordlessly he held out the dress and gave it an imperious little twitch.

Molly snatched it from his hand. "Bully," she muttered, and stomped into the dressing room. The dress fit like a crayon wrapper, too. It clung to her breasts and her hips when she shimmied into it. But once she had it on, it highlighted every curve. It also swished softly when she walked, making her aware of its fluid drape and keeping her from rocking back on her heels and shoving her hands in her pockets—because like all the others it didn't have any pockets!—the way she did when she was working on an engine.

And that, she supposed, was the general idea.

Still, it seemed very plain, very simple. She said so. "And it doesn't have a back, either."

"I noticed," Joaquin said drily. "Simple is good. You don't need frills and flounces," he told her. "Those are for women who need to draw the eye away from who they are. You, *querida,* have all the natural assets you need."

His words—and the way he was looking at her—made her

warm all over. Made her feel attractive. Enticing. Some of that power she'd felt the night before bubbled up again inside her.

It was scary. Invigorating. Maybe a little bit dangerous.

Like playing with fire.

Carson, she reminded herself. *Think about Carson.*

It was like putting a damper on the flames.

But only for the moment. When she had chosen all her purchases and Joaquin picked up the pile of carrier bags, then offered her his arm, she hesitated only briefly.

This was a lesson, she assured herself. Only a lesson.

"Bueno," Joaquin approved. "Now come along. We will get something to eat and then I will let you flirt with me."

Only a lesson, she repeated desperately as a light breeze off the sea ruffled through her newly cut hair. It teased her, tickled her, challenged her.

Last night's power was definitely back. Now she needed to learn how to harness it, control it, use it.

She took a deep breath and nodded, then fluttered her lashes outrageously at him. "I'll give it my best shot."

HER BEST SHOT damned near did him in.

Well, maybe that was an exaggeration.

But the new haircut not only did wonders for her looks, it seemed to jump-start her self-confidence. From her fluttering lashes to her twinkling eyes to her impish grin to her glossy cap of auburn hair, Molly McGillivray was a bundle of temptation.

And Joaquin was not immune.

On the contrary, he was as susceptible as the next man. More so, perhaps, because he enjoyed it so much.

He played his part enthusiastically, relishing the banter, the innuendo, the wicked teasing. It was a sort of verbal foreplay, he supposed. A prelude to things to come.

But for the moment he was content just to watch her eat, to smile as she tossed her head and ran her fingers experimentally through her newly shorn locks, to offer her a piece of his steak and feel the burn of desire as she nibbled it off the end of his fork.

After they'd eaten, he drank a cup of coffee and she ordered dessert.

"Something really decadent," she decided, studying the menu. "Ah, yes. I'll have the Sinful Seduction," she told the waiter, making his eyes grow wide and Joaquin choke on his coffee.

Molly grinned at him as the waiter left. "It's just chocolate cake," she explained. "But it sounds much more wicked than that. Perfect, don't you think?"

Joaquin nodded, not quite able to speak.

When it arrived, she gave him a bite of it. It was very good, but not as good as the tiny smidgen of whipped cream he removed from above her upper lip moments later.

She jerked at his touch, then her tongue darted out to run over the spot he'd just touched, and he sucked in his breath.

"What's wrong?" Molly demanded.

"Nothing." Nothing that a little sexual satisfaction wouldn't resolve.

"Do I have more gunk on my face?" She patted at her lips and chin.

"You're fine," he said.

"Am I boring you? Of course I'm boring you," she answered her own question. She shoved the plate of cake aside. "We can go. I've had enough. I—"

"No!" He caught her hand and kept her from rising. "Finish your dessert. Please. Or," he said as the thought occurred to him, "give me another bite."

She started to push the plate toward him, then stopped and drew it back toward her and picked up the fork. "All right," she said slowly. "We'll share."

She picked up a piece on the fork and held it out to him. He took it, savored it, all the while watching as she took another forkful and put it in her own mouth. There was a crumb on her lip. He ached to nibble it off. She ran her tongue over it, then offered him another bite, her eyes never leaving his.

It was the most erotic piece of cake he'd ever eaten.

It was sinful seduction right down to the last crumb.

And then when he was giving serious consideration to offering her a further lesson in a hotel room nearby, she glanced at her watch and yelped, "Ohmigod, I'm late!"

He frowned, confused. There was no timetable for seduction. In that way it was even better than soccer. "Late?"

"I told Sophy we'd meet them at four. *You* told Sophy we'd meet them!" She was jumping to her feet and grabbing for the carrier bags even as she spoke. "It's already ten past. Hugh will have my head. We have to be punctual. Reliable. Professional," she quoted. "I shouldn't have done this!"

"Sophy will understand. You can tell her our flying lesson took longer than we thought." He grinned, but she just shook her head. She was picking up the bill and fumbling for her purse.

Annoyed, Joaquin snatched the bill from her hand, glanced at it, tossed some bills on the table, then took the carrier bags from her.

"I will carry them," he told her, more annoyed than he wanted to admit at her ability to switch gears so quickly, to think about Hugh and her job and the rest of the world when he was still thinking about only her. "And you *should* have done this," he said firmly.

But he was talking to her back. Molly was already running out the door.

IF THE REACTIONS of the male population of Pelican Cay was anything to go by when they saw Molly that evening, her new haircut was a raving success.

Hoby the boatman gaped when she poked her head out of the plane. "Who you be?" he demanded, making her laugh delightedly as his astonishment turned to an admiring grin.

Then Amby Higgs dropped his soda bottle on the dock at the sight of her. And Jimmy Cash's jaw nearly dragged on the ground. The men playing dominoes under the tree by the customs house couldn't seem to take their eyes off her.

Nathan Wolfe did a double-take as he came out of the grocery store. "Molly?" he said as if he didn't believe his eyes.

"Hi, Nath," Molly called cheerfully. "How you doin'?"

"Fine, thanks," Nathan replied, then, looking her up and down, grinned his approval. "Obviously so are you."

Molly blushed but looked pleased. "It's pretty amazing," she said to Joaquin as they continued up the hill. "I didn't think anyone would notice."

"They noticed," Joaquin said grimly. And they could damned well stuff their eyeballs back into their heads. He scowled at every last one of them. And when they finally got back to her place and she opened the gate, he said flatly, "I'm coming in."

She didn't demur, but led the way up the steps and opened the door. "Just drop them on the sofa," she said, waving an arm toward it. "I'll sort them out later." She was opening her purse as she spoke and taking some money out of her wallet. She held it out to him. "Thank you," she said politely. "For today."

He stared at her, then, appalled, at the money in her hand. "What's that for?"

"Lunch."

"When I invite a woman out for a meal, I pay the bill!"

"But you didn't invite me. You just said, 'We'll go eat and you can flirt with me.'" She quoted him exactly. And infuriatingly.

"It was an invitation," he said through his teeth. "And now is the lesson. You will be polite enough to accept it."

The corners of her mouth twitched. "Do you know, the only time you sound Spanish in the least is when you're coming over all bossy and arrogant?"

"I can be bossy and arrogant, as you call it—" he bit out

"—in any language I choose. And you can be polite in English."

They glared at each other. She thrust the money at him. He folded his arms across his chest.

Finally she—and it would have had to be her because he was not giving an inch—sighed and stuffed the money back in her wallet. "Fine. Have it your way."

He nodded curtly, still incensed. "I will."

Their gazes held. The awareness between them grew. The need. The desire. Everything that had been building like a summer storm all afternoon.

Mesmerized, Joaquin lifted a hand to touch her hair. It was like silk against his skin. Slowly, gently he threaded his fingers through it, let them graze her scalp. She went totally still under his touch, didn't even seem to breathe as his fingers skimmed lightly over the bones of her head, then ruffled the hair against her ears.

"Que bonita eres," he murmured. *"Bellisima."*

He heard her swallow, could see the pulse flutter in her neck. Deliberately he trailed a finger along the line of her jaw to her chin. He touched her mouth.

She jerked, as if out of a sleep, and took a quick step back. "Wow. That's pretty powerful stuff."

Joaquin frowned. "Powerful stuff?"

"Spanish compliments," Molly said with a light laugh. "Is that part of your regular routine?"

"Routine?" He practically growled the word.

She gave herself a little shake. "You know, the seduction bit. Is that what you say to all the girls?" She had moved away from him now, had put the coffee table between them.

"I don't have a 'seduction bit,'" he told her sharply.

"No? It's all improvised, then?"

He scowled. "What is this? Why are you angry?" He watched her pacing around on the other side of the room and wanted to go to her and grab her and make her tell him what was going on.

"I'm not angry." Her tone said otherwise, though. "I'm just…putting things in perspective." She hugged her arms across her chest.

"What does that mean, in perspective?"

No, she was definitely not like all the other women he'd charmed and flirted with this month. They had been as predictable as the tides. This woman was a complete puzzlement.

She shook her head. "It means I'm trying to keep my head," she said. "You make me crazy."

"*I?* I make *you* crazy!" Joaquin gave a harsh laugh. "Do you know what you make me? You make me want to do this!"

And he took two steps, went straight over the coffee table, hauled her into his arms and kissed her.

Goooooooaaaaaaalllllll!

Yes, oh dear lord, yes.

Just like in soccer, it wasn't all in the setup. It wasn't all in the finesse. Sometimes it was just a matter of desperation. You saw a little bit of daylight. You knew what you had to do. You took the risk.

And the kiss.

It was explosive, hungry, powerful. There was nothing careful, nothing practiced, nothing schooled about it. It was all improvisation, Molly would have said, Joaquin thought, if Molly could have said anything.

But she couldn't because she was completely occupied, her mouth meeting his, her tongue tangling with his, tasting his, kissing him with an eagerness equal to his own, driving him further, so that his hands slid down her back to cup her buttocks and pull her against him, so he could feel her soft yielding body against the hard aching need of his.

It was exhilarating. It was heart-poundingly wonderful.

And it was over—just like that.

Somehow—he wasn't even sure how—when he'd loosed his grip to haul her closer, she'd slipped away and skittered right across the room, where she stood, ruffling her fingers through her mussed hair and taking quick, shallow little breaths.

"Well," she said, blinking rapidly. "That was interesting."

He gaped at her. *"Interesting?"* He practically strangled on the word.

"Instructive," she modified, her tone as cheery as an elementary schoolteacher's. "And perhaps a very good place to end today's lesson." She gave him a bright smile. "We wouldn't want me to get information overload, now would we?"

CHAPTER FOUR

SHE WAS the one-day wonder of Pelican Cay.

At least, Molly hoped her fame—or notoriety, depending on how you looked at it—didn't last any longer than that.

By the next morning almost everyone on the island had dropped by Fly Guy to see for themselves. Several people had been hanging around the shop when she arrived to open up in the morning. More showed up when they left. More stopped in to chat and ogle later in the day.

"Maybe you should just announce my new look on the radio," Molly finally said when even Trina the weather girl turned up.

Trina laughed. "No point. Everybody already knows. It's yesterday's news."

Molly devoutly hoped so. She didn't want to think about it.

She had bigger things on her mind. Like the way she'd responded to Joaquin Santiago's kiss.

She refused to think of the kiss as anything more than a "lesson." She understood perfectly well what he was doing. He was rattling her, waking her up, making her aware of how little she really knew.

What he probably didn't have any clue about was how much she *wanted* to know! And, unfortunately, how much her desires focused on him.

She felt guilty about it. As if she were being unfaithful to Carson. And it didn't help when Hugh got back from Miami, walked in the shop, took one look at her and his jaw dropped. "God almighty, look at you!"

Then he walked all the way around her, shaking his head in wordless amazement while Molly bristled, expecting brotherly sarcasm. What she got was a brotherly narrowing of eyes and the suspicious demand, "Is this on account of Santiago?"

"No! Of course not! How can you say such a thing?"

"You were with him the other night. Syd said he went with you to Nassau yesterday."

"He went with the group," Molly corrected, which was technically true even though actually Hugh was the more accurate.

Her brother grunted, unconvinced. "Well, just be careful. He's not the settling-down kind. And he makes women forget their common sense."

"What?"

"I'm only warning you. You don't want to get dumped by some Spanish playboy, Mol'."

"Excuuuuuuse me?"

Her indignation seemed to finally get through to him because he shuffled awkwardly. "I just meant, he's out of your league. He eats little girls like you for breakfast."

"I can take care of myself, thank you very much," Molly said hotly and hoped it was the truth. "And anyway, you seem to have forgotten Carson."

"Carson?" The blank look on Hugh's face told her that he had indeed forgotten Carson.

"I am engaged to Carson," Molly reminded him. "I've been engaged to Carson for years. Just because we haven't set a date doesn't mean we aren't getting married."

"Oh, right." Hugh looked almost comically relieved.

Molly didn't know whether to laugh or cry, especially when later that afternoon she had a virtually identical conversation with Lachlan.

He came to the field every day for soccer practice. But today he stopped by the shop first. "Got a minute?"

She was working on one of the mokes they rented to tourists, but she stopped and looked up. "Sure."

He studied her for a moment. "Nice haircut."

"Thanks." She smiled, relieved he wasn't going to lecture her the way Hugh had.

"It's nice to see you looking like a, um...girl for a change." He cracked his knuckles loudly.

Molly weighed the wrench in her hand.

"You clean up good," he went on. "But I...I just don't want you getting your hopes up."

"What," Molly said slowly, "are you talking about?"

"Santiago." Lachlan stuffed his hands into the pockets of his shorts and rocked back on his heels. "He's a great guy," he went on rapidly. "A good friend. One of the best. But he's not going to look twice—"

"Stop," Molly said. "Right there." She stood up.

"I just—"

"Stop." She came around the moke and stood nose-to-nose with him. "What I do and who I see—and who I have a drink with or go to dinner with or go to bed with—"

"You went to bed with him?" Lachlan was apoplectic.

"I did not go to bed with him! But it wouldn't be your business if I had. I'm an adult, Lachlan. I can do what I like with whomever I like. I do have certain standards, however," she said, as much to remind herself of the fact as to remind him. "And I do not dally with other men when I am engaged to be married."

It took more seconds than Molly would have liked for the penny to drop.

When it did, Lachlan blinked rapidly then grinned widely. "Son of a gun," he said. "I forgot about Carson."

So for a few brief moments had she. Thank God her brain had reengaged last night before her body did something she would forever regret.

"Well, don't forget Carson," she said firmly, then gave her

brother a smile of saccharine sweetness. "Now, is there anything else?"

"Guess not." He grinned crookedly, then reached out and ruffled her hair. "Heck of a haircut, Mol'. Carson's gonna love it."

She hoped so. She wished—dear God, she wished!—that he would come home and love it—love *her!*—right now!

Two days ago the ten days until his arrival had seemed far too short a time for all the things she needed to learn. Now the eight days still to go seemed like forever.

And how was she going to keep her mind on Carson when a certain black-haired devil was—just as Hugh had predicted—robbing her of her common sense?

PART OF WINNING was strategy.

It was having a plan. Knowing who the other side was. Sizing up the competition.

"Lachlan in?" Joaquin gave Suzette, Lachlan's assistant, his best charming smile.

She smiled back. "He just got in from soccer practice. He's on the phone but he won't be long. Go on in."

Ordinarily Joaquin would have come back later. He steered clear of Lachlan during soccer practice so he didn't have to deal with his friend's well-meaning but misguided attempts to get him involved. But today he had his own agenda, and that was more important.

Lachlan, still wearing the shorts and T-shirt he coached in, looked sweaty and disheveled as he beckoned Joaquin in, finished his conversation, then hung up, leaned back in his chair and grinned at his friend.

"Come to sign up?" he asked. "I could still use an offensive coach."

"No, thanks. Not interested," Joaquin said firmly. He cast around for a way to lead into what he wanted to ask, a casual indifferent way to get answers. There wasn't one. Finally he just asked straight-out.

"Who's this guy Molly's engaged to?"

Lachlan blinked. "Carson? What about him?"

"Just curious. I didn't know she was engaged. Never heard her mention him. And then we were talking the other day and his name came up. She said he was some big shot who'd grown up here. I just wondered why—Pelican Cay being a pretty small place—I'd never met him." There. That sounded avuncular enough.

"Because Carson's never here," Lachlan said. "He's on his way to running the world."

Joaquin was surprised to hear that. The wife of a world ruler didn't sound like the sort of thing Molly would aspire to become. He flung himself down in one of the armchairs in Lachlan's office. "Go on."

Lachlan leaned back and steepled his fingers on his chest. "I guess you could call him a big shot now. But he sure as hell wasn't when we were growing up. He was a fisherman's son. Skip Sawyer drowned when Carson was fifteen. He'd just started fishing full-time with his dad—and then he was on his own. Some of the others offered to buy him out, take over the boat. His mother tried to talk him into it. But Carson wouldn't do it. Said he was going to do what his old man had done—and then some." A smile touched Lachlan's mouth as he remembered. "And he did just that. He worked his tail off. Saved his money. Couple of the old men crewed for him in the early days. By the time he was eighteen he had enough to buy another boat and hire another crew. But he never forgot the old men who helped him out. He takes care of them now."

So, Carson Sawyer was energetic, determined, hardworking, frugal and loyal. A regular paragon.

"He owns a fleet now," Lachlan said. "And real estate in the islands and partnerships in a couple of businesses in the States. Last time I saw him he was talking to me about diversification and taking some of his business to Europe and the South Pacific. No end to his ambition. But he's never forgotten his roots. He's a helluva guy. The sort of man you want to ride out a storm with.''

No weaknesses at all, then. Carson Flaming Sawyer was well nigh perfect. Except for needing to wake up where Molly was concerned.

"I hear you had a drink with Molly the other night," Lachlan said. He wasn't lounging back in his chair anymore. He was sitting up straight, leaning forward, looking intently at Joaquin.

Joaquin sat up straighter, too. "That's right. I did.''

There was a long silence. Their gazes met. Lachlan's eyes were a different color—brilliant blue to Molly's deep green. But the intensity was the same. The challenge.

"I like your sister," Joaquin said evenly. "She's terrific."

"She is. But she's not a woman of the world."

"What's that supposed to mean?"

"It means don't mess with her."

Joaquin's jaw locked. "Seems to me it's Carson Sawyer who's messing with her."

Lachlan frowned. "How so?"

"If he's engaged to her, why isn't he here? Why hasn't he been here? Why isn't he setting a date for their wedding?"

"I don't think that's for me to say," Lachlan replied. "And if you were to ask either him or Molly you might get a bloody nose for your trouble." His gaze narrowed. "Or have you asked her?"

"No." Which was true. He hadn't asked. Molly had told him. "I just wondered."

"I imagine they'll set a date when they're ready," Lachlan said. His mouth quirked into a grin. "Maybe the new haircut will inspire him."

Joaquin's fingers clenched. "Maybe. There ought to be more to it than that, though."

Lachlan's brows lifted. "Since when did you become patron saint of the perennially engaged?"

Joaquin stood up and flexed his shoulders. "We talked. I wondered. That's all."

"As long as that's all it stays." Lachlan's words were mild, but the warning was clear enough. He stood up and grabbed the towel he'd dried off with after soccer practice. "I need a shower. You want to come back to the house with me? Fiona will feed you."

"No." He paused. "Thanks."

As they went out the door, Lachlan clapped him on the shoulder. "Molly's a good kid. Carson's a good guy. They'll make a good match of it. And probably soon. They just need to wait until the time is right. Don't worry about it." He slanted a grin in Joaquin's direction as they stood in the inn's foyer. "If you're in a matchmaking frame of mind, maybe it's time you found a woman of your own."

"I've got my mother to do that for me," Joaquin said.

Lachlan laughed. "Well, ring her and tell her to get busy."

"She already is. Why do you think I'm hiding out here?"

"Rough life," Lachlan said cheerfully. Then his grin vanished and he looked quite serious. "Are you doing okay?" he asked. "I mean we haven't talked much. I figured you'd sort things out on your own, but if you need anything—"

"I'm fine." Joaquin cut him off. "Go get your shower. I'll see you around."

Lachlan hesitated, then shrugged and punched Joaquin lightly in the abs.

"Don't do anything I didn't do," he said and, with a wave of farewell in Suzette's direction, he loped out the door and headed home.

Joaquin watched him go, aware that he'd already done something Lachlan hadn't done—and certainly wouldn't approve of him doing. He'd kissed Molly. And he'd have happily done a damn sight more than that.

He rubbed his hands down his face, feeling suddenly weary. Then slowly he climbed the stairs to his room.

SHE DIDN'T SEE JOAQUIN all day, which was fine.

Or all the day after that either, which was still okay, but distracting because she wondered if he was avoiding her. Or if she was avoiding him.

And try as she might, she couldn't come up with any answers. It was probably one of those approach-avoidance things she'd studied about in psychology. Or maybe it was an approach-approach thing. Or maybe—

Maybe, Molly thought irritably, she was just losing her mind.

She paced her living room trying to decide whether to call him or not. It wasn't as if she expected to be the focus of his every waking moment. She definitely didn't *want* to be the focus of his every waking moment.

But when a man kissed a woman like Joaquin had kissed her—as if he'd wanted to do a lot more than kiss her—then the woman was just sort of, well, curious about where things might go from there.

Might being the operative word. In fact, Molly knew, they weren't going anywhere. She didn't want them to. She was engaged to Carson. And even if she weren't, things still wouldn't go anywhere because Joaquin Santiago was not a man for marrying.

Still, she thought as she paced, she wanted to see him, to talk to him. To kiss him.

Oh, God, where had that come from?

She needed to stop thinking about him. Or else, she thought quite suddenly, she needed to do more than think about him. She needed to see him, to desensitize herself to him. To spend more time with him.

Kiss him.

She groaned and closed her eyes. But the memories that plagued her as soon as she did that were vivid and all too realistic. She could, with very little effort, remember every single detail of the time his mouth had been on hers. The kiss was imprinted on her brain. It couldn't possibly have been as hungry and demanding as she remembered it.

Could it?

Maybe she needed to find out.

"DINNER? AT YOUR PLACE?" Joaquin repeated her invitation cautiously, still surprised that it had been Molly's voice he'd heard when he'd picked up his ringing phone.

"I just thought it would be a good way to say thank you," she said breezily. "For all you did for me the other day, you know?"

He wasn't sure what "all you did" encompassed. The haircut? The shopping spree? The lunch? The *kiss?*

And depending on which, then what?

Like getting the ball and taking his shot, in a single instant his brain raced through a hundred possibilities.

And went, as usual, with his gut instinct. "I'd like that, yes."

It sounded as if she let out her breath quickly before she answered. "Great. I'll see you about seven, then."

"I'll be there."

DON'T DO ANYTHING I didn't do.

Joaquin repeated Lachlan's words over and over in his mind as he chose a bottle of wine, bought some flowers and headed toward Molly's house.

At least, he assured himself, he went with the best of intentions. He was helping a woman in need. Tutoring her in the fine art of making a man aware of her. Imparting age-old knowledge about the flirtatious give-and-take between the sexes that she had somehow missed out on.

And if he just happened to make her aware that there were other fish in the sea than Carson Sawyer, well then, she didn't love Sawyer very much, did she?

It wasn't as if he was intending to have his wicked way with her.

He wasn't. He was just helping her discover her Inner Woman, and pointing out—only if she was interested—that there were other options. It was a good deed on his part. Not self-interest.

It wasn't as if he wanted her for himself.

She was fun to be with. Exhilarating. And kissing her made his toes curl and his body want to do far more than that.

But Molly was not his sort of woman. She wanted marriage. Permanence. A home. A family. *Babies,* for heaven's sake!

Not to mention another man.

Well, they'd see about that last, he thought as he bounded up the steps and knocked on the screen door.

"Come on in." Her voice floated back from the kitchen.

Marvelous spicy smells wafted toward him, making his stomach growl appreciatively. He pushed open the screen and followed his nose into the kitchen…and forgot all about the hunger in his stomach as another very basic hunger—for her, regardless of all his previous pious denial—shoved it out of the way.

Molly was standing barefoot at the stove scooping rice from a pot into a blue crockery bowl. She was wearing one of the sundresses she'd bought yesterday. It was a riot of reds and oranges, what there was of it, and by rights it should have clashed with her hair. But in fact the dress complemented it as well as bringing out the golden tan on her bare back. He swallowed hard.

She turned at the sound of his footsteps, and her face was flushed from the heat of the kitchen, and the color it added to her cheeks made her lovelier than ever.

"You look…fantastic," he told her.

She grinned. "Because you have good taste. It is sort of cool, isn't it?" She twirled around, making the skirt flare out, giving him a glimpse of long, tanned legs as well.

"Very cool," he managed. "Here." He thrust a bouquet at her.

"Flowers?" A smile of both surprise and delight lit her face. "No one's ever given me flowers before."

Take that, Sawyer, Joaquin thought grimly.

He hadn't intended to bring them, either, but as he'd passed the Pineapple Shop, a riot of blossoms had caught his eye and he'd stopped and bought them for her.

She sniffed them, then smiled appreciatively. "They're lovely. Thank you."

"My pleasure," he said gruffly.

He handed her the wine and discovered no one had ever brought her wine before either. She asked him to open it and pour it while she dished up the meal. It was all very civilized, very proper. She didn't need lessons in this department, that was for sure.

"Sit down," she invited him.

He sat at the kitchen table, which she had set very nicely with colorful mats and bright island stoneware. She took a seat opposite him and smiled. "I'm so glad you could come."

It was another one of those defining moments, but he was damned if he could figure out what had been defined. He nodded and took a careful breath. "Me, too."

Molly McGillivray didn't need cooking lessons either. The food was wonderful. The wine, by sheer good luck, complemented it perfectly, dry and cold and smooth. They enjoyed both. The conversation was casual and enjoyable, too.

She told him about the banner she had agreed to make for the homecoming festival. She raved about the number of charters Hugh had lined up bringing groups in for the various events and activities. It was a big boost for the business, she said. For all the island businesses. There were no rooms available anywhere.

Joaquin let her talk, simply enjoying the meal and the moment and, most of all, the woman. It was all very straightforward. Not flirtatious at all.

Which meant what? That the kiss they'd shared, which had

pretty nearly taken the top of his head off, had been simply academically interesting to her?

No. Not possible. He'd felt her heart hammering against his chest. He'd tasted her passion. He'd felt the heat of her mouth on his.

"Fiona says he's obsessing about it," Molly was saying.

He jerked back to the moment. "Obsessing?" he echoed, not sure who or what she was talking about. *He* was the one who was obsessing—about that kiss!

"Lachlan," Molly said. "About the soccer tournament. The kids are in a single elimination tournament. Ten teams from various islands all coming here. And Lachlan is a basket case."

"He would be," Joaquin nodded, dragging his mind back to the moment, even if it had to do with soccer. "That's Lachlan."

"I'm glad, actually. It'll keep him busy. Less time for him to be fretting about me."

"What about you?"

"My haircut makes him nervous. How stupid is that?" Molly shook her head in despair.

Not stupid at all, Joaquin thought. But he didn't say anything and he certainly didn't tell her about his conversation with her brother. He picked up the wine bottle. "More?"

"No, I'm fine." She pushed her plate aside, but she didn't stand up or offer him a cup of coffee. Instead she smiled lazily at him.

Joaquin felt a lick of desire but controlled it. Tonight he would go slow. Tonight he would teach her step by step the dance of seduction between a man and a woman. Tipping back in his chair, he cocked his head slightly, watching her from beneath slumberous lids.

It was a deliberate move, calculated to make her aware of how a heated gaze and simple silence could heat the blood.

A bare foot slid up his leg.

"Jesus!" He jerked upright, his heart jumping, his chair banging all four feet on the floor.

"What's wrong?" Molly was sitting up straight now, too, looking equal parts worried and chagrined. "Did I do it wrong?"

She'd done it *on purpose?*

He swore in Spanish and when that didn't seem sufficient, he moved on to Catalan. And even when he was finished swearing, he could still feel the tingle from the line her toes had drawn on his calf. His heart still slammed.

"Joaquin?"

"It's all right," he said through his teeth. "You just…surprised me."

"Oh. I thought—" She stopped, chewed on her lower lip, then said, "Maybe if I warned you first?"

"Warned me?" He choked out the words.

"I should have told you. I thought you wouldn't mind if we practiced a bit."

He was speechless. She wanted to *practice* running her toes up the inside of his leg? He made a strangled sound.

"Do you mind?"

And how the hell did he answer that? *Don't do anything I didn't do.* Oh, yeah, sure. No possibility Lachlan had let Molly do anything like this!

But he wasn't Lachlan. He wasn't Molly McGillivray's brother. And those toes of hers were the most erotic damned toes he'd ever felt in his life.

"Go ahead," he said tightly, and steeled himself for a heart attack.

She settled into her chair again, smiled across the table at him again. He held his breath, listened to the pound of his heart as soft tentative toes touched his calf.

Even forewarned, Joaquin wasn't as controlled as he wanted to be. He held himself rigid and unbreathing as the toes traveled slowly up his calf, drew tiny circles on the inside of his knee, made him suck in his breath when they reached them hem of his shorts. Made him want them to move up higher.

They slid back down again.

"How was that?" Molly wanted to know.

His brain was turning to mush. All the blood that wasn't digesting his dinner was busy pooling elsewhere.

"Terrific," he said through clenched teeth.

"Do you think I should slide them or walk them?" She frowned as she considered this, then demonstrated.

This time the toes tickled their way up his calf onto his inner thigh. His whole leg jerked. "I think, ah—" He *couldn't* think! "—the slide," he managed, sounding as if someone had hold of his windpipe. "The slide is better."

"You think so?" She did it again experimentally. Slid her foot lightly up his leg, reached his knee, moved her toes lightly along the inside of his thigh.

"Yesssss." The word hissed between his teeth.

"Oh, good. Excellent. It works." Molly looked like she'd just got a new toy. She leaned toward him eagerly. "What shall we do now?"

Joaquin knew what he wanted to do. He shut his eyes and prayed for strength. "The dishes."

CHAPTER FIVE

"DISHES?" Molly echoed, sounding stricken.

"Dishes," Joaquin repeated grimly, shoving back his chair and getting to his feet just a little painfully.

They did the dishes. She washed; he dried.

And he cursed himself for a fool the whole time. Why the hell wasn't he taking her to bed? Stripping off that delightful dress? Running his toes up *her* thigh? Discovering the secrets of her body? Making hot sweet passionate love to her?

It was obviously what she was angling for. There was no question that it was what *he* wanted!

Still, he couldn't do it.

No, correction. He *could* do it. Hell, yes, he could!

But he *wouldn't* do it, damn this idiotic perverse streak of honorable behavior he hadn't even known he had. Because that was what it was, he thought, banging the dishes into the cupboard with controlled fury. He couldn't make love to her when she didn't know what she was doing.

She didn't know, or she wouldn't be winding him up this way, wouldn't be teasing and tempting and all but throwing herself at him, then discussing it as if it were strategy for winning a game!

It didn't matter that he saw seduction in exactly those terms. This wasn't seduction! This was—

His fists clenched in the dish towel. His hands strangled it. His mind grappled with forming the word.

Love?

It took him ages to get it out. As four-letter words went, it wasn't one that generally sprang to his lips. He had trouble even bending his mind around it. In fact his mind rejected it, said, Don't be ridiculous. And probably he was being— Probably it was nothing more than his fevered brain in the heat of the moment, trying to rationalize the irrationalizable.

It was just that he'd never *not* gone to bed with a willing woman. Not one he *wanted* to go to bed with, anyway.

It was perverse. It was infuriating. It was unnatural!

He flung the dish towel on the counter even as the dishes in the drainer piled up. "I have to go."

Beside him Molly hunched her shoulders and kept on washing. "Go, then." She didn't look his way.

"Damn it, Molly, you can't just cold-bloodedly make a man want you!"

"Apparently not," she said bitterly.

Was she blinking back tears? Joaquin clenched his fists to keep from reaching for her, wrapping her in his arms. *Dios mio,* what if he made her cry?

"*¡Lo siento! No te llores.* Don't cry! I'm sorry, Molly. *¡De veras!* Honest! I just can't—*we* can't! I just…need to go."

She whirled to face him, her cheeks scarlet. "Then damn it to hell, just go! Get out of here!" And she shoved past him and ran up the stairs. A second later her bedroom door slammed so hard the dishes rattled on the shelves.

He just stood there in the silent aftermath, wanting to go after her, wanting to make it better, knowing damned well that if he did, he would only make it worse.

Silently he stared at the dishes left in the drainer, then picked up the dish towel again. He could dry them, he supposed. But, like everything else tonight, it might be smarter to leave them unfinished.

Lachlan never did them, he thought with grim humor as his friend's words echoed in his head. He tossed the towel on the counter, turned and walked out of the house.

Don't do anything I didn't do. He could hear the words now as he went down the steps. He could see Lachlan's wry grin as he'd said them. But more clearly he could see Molly's furious tear-streaked face.

His mouth twisted. *Don't do anything I didn't do.*

"Don't worry," he said bitterly as he let himself out the gate. "I didn't."

HE NEEDED TO FIND a woman. A willing, eager, no-strings-attached woman. A woman who didn't try to seduce him while she had her sights set on marrying another man.

One night of unconditional sex and he'd be fine, Joaquin assured himself. Words like *love* wouldn't even occur to him. And they sure as hell wouldn't come wrapped in a package like Molly McGillivray.

A man on a mission, he headed straight for the Grouper, grabbed a cold beer from Michael, the bartender, and surveyed the crop of available women with an eye toward plucking the most appealing and taking her back to his room as soon as possible.

One of them, a British girl called Charlotte, seemed to feel the same way. She caught his eye—or he caught hers—halfway across the room. It was easy enough to pick up his beer and saunter her way. Easier still to make small talk with her, discover she knew exactly who he was—"that footballer they call the Casanova of the pitch." She giggled, batted her lashes and ran a finger down his cheek.

Her touch was not nearly as tempting as Molly's toes had been, in fact it did nothing at all. But sometimes these things took time, he told himself, conveniently forgetting that they never had before.

He gave her an encouraging wink even as he said, "That's just tabloid journalism. You know what they're like."

Charlotte gave another giggle. "My mum always says, where there's smoke, there's fire."

"Does she?" Joaquin settled on a bar stool and tried to muster up some enthusiasm.

"Oh, yes." Charlotte gave a seductive little wiggle that

gave him a view of several more inches of bare thigh. "I've been wondering if it's true." Big blue eyes met his.

Charlotte could have flirted for England, and he was feeling reckless enough to go along with it. She was staying at the Moonstone, too. And she was—amazing, wasn't it?—very happy to walk back with him when he was ready to leave.

They climbed the stairs to their rooms together.

In minutes, he thought, he could have her naked in his bed.

It had absolutely no appeal. He gave his head a hard shake. Dear God, what was wrong with him tonight?

"I think I'm getting sick," he muttered.

"Oooh, poor darling," she put a hand on his forehead. "You should go to bed." There was a purr in her voice. It meant she didn't expect him to go there alone.

"You're right. I should," Joaquin said. He stuck his key in the door and opened it. "Good night."

Charlotte stared, nonplussed. "Good night?" she squeaked.

He nodded. Then because none of it was her fault, he gave her a bleak smile. "Thanks for coming back with me. I appreciate it."

"I could come in with you," she suggested. "Put a cool washcloth on your forehead. Make you feel better."

His mouth twisted. "*Gracias, no.* I don't think that'll fix it."

A cold shower and soaking his head didn't fix it either. Drowning himself might. He considered it. He considered a lot of things—none of which made any sense and all of which had to do with a certain redhead he couldn't get out of his mind. And he was just about ready to stalk back across the island and let her have her wicked way with him when the phone rang.

He snatched it up, hoping against hope that it was Molly, though God knew why she would call him. He was the one who walked out on her. "H'lo?"

"*Ah, mi hijo. Bueno. ¿Te vas bien?*"

Joaquin nearly dropped the phone. "Papa?" He squinted

at his watch. "It's—" he did a quick mental calculation "—five in the morning. What's wrong?"

"Nothing is wrong, *mi hijo*. And it is not five in the morning. It is eleven, same as you. We are in New York."

"New York?"

"Which you would know," Martin Santiago went on smoothly, "if you had read the papers I sent you. Or if you'd called your mother more often."

"I've been…busy." And in no mood to read papers about the business even though he'd spent the month trying to come to terms with going into it.

"What are you doing in New York?" he asked his father.

"I will tell you later," Martin said. "In person."

"You want me to come to New York?"

"No, no," his father said cheerfully. "We are coming to Pelican Cay."

"*What?*"

"To have a little holiday, *sí?* And to complicate your life." His father laughed.

"To complicate—"

"You always told us what a wonderful place it is!" Martin went on. "Lachlan, too. Remember how he always invites us to visit."

Joaquin remembered, but even as he did, his mind reeled. "You mean soon? It's really a madhouse right now, Papa. They're having a homecoming celebration, like an island fiesta. There's a lot going on. Way too many people. Not a good time for a holiday. I'll be home soon and—"

"We know all about the fiesta. Your mother read about it on the internet. A wonderful thing the internet, *sí?*"

"*Sí,*" Joaquin said dully. He pinched the bridge of his nose. "It's a little island, Papa. There are only a few places to stay."

"We stay with Lachlan."

"With *Lachlan? Lachlan* invited you?"

Mr. Don't Do Anything I Didn't Do? By God, Joaquin would kill him!

"No, no. Not Lachlan. Fiona invited us! Such a lovely girl. So friendly."

"Yeah, real friendly," Joaquin agreed wearily.

"Your mother talked to her this afternoon when Lachlan was at soccer practice. She says he has a team." His father sounded jovial and tolerantly amused at a grown man still involved in what he'd always considered a child's game. But it was okay for Lachlan to do it. Lachlan wasn't his son, wasn't expected to go into the family business.

"We are looking forward to meeting her," Martin said. "We will see you Thursday."

The day after tomorrow?

"Papa—"

"Hasta entonces, mi hijo."

"¡Espérate, Papa! Wait a sec—"

But his father had hung up.

Joaquin flung himself back on the bed and stared at the ceiling. His parents? Coming here? To do what? Complicate his life?

It was almost—but not quite—enough to make him forget one particular redheaded problem.

"You don't need to complicate my life, Papa," he muttered. It was already complicated enough.

"I CAN'T BELIEVE you agreed to let them come!"

The last time he was in Lachlan's office, it had seemed a whole lot bigger. This morning it felt like a tiny cage—and Joaquin felt trapped.

"I was supposed to call them back and say, don't come? After all the hospitality they've shown me? Besides, Fiona invited them." Lachlan was totally unsympathetic as he leaned back in his leather desk chair while his gaze followed Joaquin pacing around the room.

"You could have said she'd made a mistake, you didn't have any place available."

"Which would have been a lie. Besides, it's no big deal."

"Not to you."

"Well, I'm sure you'll deal with it. You can't run forever."

"I'm *not* running!"

Lachlan lifted his shoulders negligently. "Sez you. Look," he said in a more conciliatory tone, "I know you needed time to get your head together after the accident. When I couldn't play anymore, I needed time, too. But you've been here a month and you haven't done a damn thing."

Except nearly go to bed with your sister. Joaquin pressed his lips into a firm line.

Lachlan, unaware, shrugged unrepentantly. "Just play it cool. Show 'em around. They'll enjoy the vacation. Besides, it's not you they're really interested in, anyway."

Joaquin frowned. "What the hell does that mean?"

"They're coming to see Duncan, not you!"

Joaquin groaned. "So I'll get the grandchildren lecture."

"They'll be too busy enjoying him to lecture you. Besides, they're bringing a couple of friends."

Joaquin stopped pacing and frowned. "What friends?"

"A couple of women your mother knows. Some widow and her daughter."

Joaquin swore fluently. "Esperanza Delgado and the lovely Marianela."

"The lovely Marianela?" Lachlan grinned. "Ah, the matchmaking mama's been hard at work."

Joaquin ground his teeth. "Looks like."

"Well, it comes to all of us sooner or later," Lachlan said with annoying good cheer.

"No one shoved Fiona down your throat," Joaquin said sharply.

Lachlan shrugged. "So go find your own woman."

The trouble was, Joaquin thought, he already had.

LIFE, MOLLY DECIDED, was a lot less complicated when you didn't try to make it go your way, when you didn't try to speed things up, control the outcome and thereby make a fool of yourself.

She'd made a fool of herself.

In her hare-brained Ms. Fix-It mode, she'd tried to turn her slow-moving engagement into a high-octane relationship. And she'd made a mess of it.

She went to work. She came home. She smiled if smiled at. She spoke if spoken to. And otherwise she kept a very low profile.

She deliberately stayed away from the Moonstone. And the Grouper. And any place else trendy and exciting. She didn't need trendy and exciting. Mostly she didn't need to run into Joaquin.

She tried not to even think about him. She was mortified every time she did! So much for trying to get him out of her system! Dear God, even now she cringed at the memory of his reaction. And her tears.

Molly McGillivray *never* cried!

Almost.

Well, she was never going to cry again. Not over a man. And not even the right man.

"Come home, Carson," she whispered into the depths of the engine she was working on. "We'll take it however you want to take it. Go as slow as you want. Just come home."

Afterward she wondered at the timing. She'd no sooner mumbled the words than the phone rang. It never failed, she thought irritably. Whenever she got up to her elbows in engine grease, the phone always rang.

Well, let it, Molly thought irritably, plunging deeper into the engine.

"People like to talk to people, not machines," Hugh maintained, which was probably true. "It's the personal touch."

But not today they wouldn't. Not if the person in question was a grumpy mechanic who'd had far too much anguish and far too little sleep. Better the answering machine get it than that she snarl and lose a potential customer. Hugh could return the call when he got back from Nassau.

But when the machine picked up, she heard, "Hey, Mol', it's Carson. Give me a call when—"

And heedless of the grease, Molly grabbed the phone. "Carson!"

"Hey! Screening your calls now? How hotshot is that?" She heard the smile in his voice—the pure, easy, normal, Carson Sawyer tone—and almost wept with gratitude.

"Hey, yourself. Hugh's in Nassau and I was working on an engine. How are you?"

"Good. Just wanted to tell you I've had a change of plans."

Molly felt her heart sink. Of course she'd basically just vowed to let him take it in his own time. But she didn't expect God to call her to account right now. "Change of plans?" she echoed.

"Yep. Thought I'd come early."

Early? Molly's heart picked itself up and dusted itself off. "Really?"

"Reckon I might fly over with Dena Wilson. You remember her? Tom's daughter."

"I remember her." Hard to forget a woman whose father owned an entire island. "Where's Dena? Is she in Savannah, too?"

"Miami mostly. But I've been working with her on a real estate deal for Tom. She's coming this weekend, too, wants to run it past her old man. She has her own plane, so I figured if I could get away, I'd fly over at the same time. Figured maybe we could talk. You said we didn't get a chance to last time I was home."

"We didn't." Her hopes lifted another notch.

"So this time we will. I've got to talk to Tom, too. He's putting together a meeting of some investors. Pretty hectic."

"But you can...fit me in?"

"Of course I can." He sounded surprised she would ask.

"And there's going to be a party at the Lodge on Saturday night," he went on. "All very upscale and ritzy from what Dena says. Formal dress. Live band. And not a steel band, either," he added with a grin. "Dancing. Ballroom, that sort of thing. I have to go. It's a command performance if I want to do business with them." His tone was apologetic.

"It's all right," Molly assured him, starting for the first time to smile. Thank you, God. "I don't mind."

"You sure?"

"I'm sure. I'll wear my new dress."

There was a split second's pause. Then Carson said, "You want to come?"

"Unless you're ashamed to be seen with me."

"No! Of course not. I'm just…surprised." He sounded stunned. "You bought a dress, Mol'? What kind of dress?"

Molly grinned. "Wait and see."

"Guess I'll have to." He sounded slightly dazed. "Do me a favor, Mol'. See if you can find me a room for the weekend. I rang the Moonstone and the Mirabelle, but they're all booked up."

"Not a problem," Molly said, recognizing an opportunity when it nearly knocked her over. "You can stay with me."

HE COULDN'T STAY holed up in his room forever. Not even to read the blasted papers his father had sent that he'd been ignoring so long. So Joaquin skimmed over them—something about a proposed merger with the place his father had apparently been visiting in New York—and tried to formulate some opinion so he could sound knowledgeable if asked.

But his heart wasn't in it and his mind wasn't on it.

He was still thinking about Molly.

He hadn't seen her since their fateful dinner, since her toe dance up his leg, since she'd run out of the room, furious with him.

He supposed he should apologize. But he didn't see that he had a damn thing to apologize for! He was the one who'd been behaving honorably. He was the one defending her virtue! From himself!

Just thinking about the injustice of it could make him furious all over again. And caroming off the wall of his room in the Moonstone didn't help. So he threw his father's papers aside, shoved Molly into the deepest corner of his mind and went out for a run.

Charlotte was just coming up from the beach. He hadn't seen her since that night, either, though she'd called his room to see if he was feeling better.

Now she said eagerly, "Want some company? I'll come with you."

But Joaquin shook his head. "Thanks. I'm fine on my own."

At least he wasn't stupid enough to drag another woman into the mess that was his life. After that first night at the Grouper when he'd thought some mindless sex would cure what ailed him, only to discover that mindless sex didn't interest him at all, he hadn't gone back to the Grouper or anywhere else.

If he could have, he'd have packed his bags and left. But with his parents showing up tomorrow afternoon, he was stuck. And of course they would just happen to have a prospective bride in their luggage.

His feet pounded along the sand. "Stuck," they said with every footfall. "Stuck, stuck, stuck, stuck, stuck."

He ran for miles. To the end of the beach, then he climbed the steps by the Mirabelle, then cut through the grounds, and when he got to the road that came back through the center of the island, he ran some more. It was hotter now. There was less breeze. Rivulets of sweat poured down his chest and back as he ran past the road to Nathan and Carin Wolfe's place. Past Lachlan's curving drive. Past the water tower and over the rise to look down on the cricket field which had, since Lachlan's return, become the soccer pitch where the team was even now practicing.

Beyond the field was Fiona's whimsical *King of the Beach* sculpture of island flotsam and jetsam. And beyond that was Fly Guy.

And Molly.

The door to the shop was open, which meant she was in there now, hard at work. He saw a flash of coppery hair pass the doorway. He stopped, attention caught.

He'd stopped in Fly Guy's offices and shop dozens of times in the past few years to arrange a flight, to talk to Hugh, to meet up with Lachlan or just shoot the breeze. Molly had always been there, in the background, busy as a beaver. He'd barely noticed.

Now he noticed nothing else.

He could stop. Say hello. Test the waters, so to speak.

Or he could run on past. Pretend the past week had never happened.

As he considered his options, he heard a shout from the field and lots of people, both kids and adults, began running in one direction, crowding around someone down on the pitch. He began walking, and picked up his pace when he saw Molly appear in the doorway, then go running toward the cluster of people.

"Call the doc," he heard. And then he heard, "Better call Hugh, too. Anybody got a mobile?"

He broke into a lope, heading across the field. "What's up?" he demanded as he came up to them and the crowd parted. Molly was kneeling next to Lachlan lying, white-faced, on the ground.

"Lachlan's broken his leg."

CHAPTER SIX

"I'M NOT GOING TO DO IT!" Joaquin was pacing the floor of the shop, cracking his knuckles, ranting, furious and, unfortunately, as gorgeous as ever, Molly thought as she stood in the doorway, bouncing Duncan in her arms.

She shouldn't be admiring his bare, muscled chest and rock-hard thighs, Molly told herself. She shouldn't be looking at him at all.

It was insane. But he was here, had followed her into the shop after Hugh and Doc Rasmussen had loaded Lachlan into the chopper, and he and Fiona, Hugh and Doc were now on their way to Nassau.

"I never said you would," she said mildly. Coach soccer, she meant. "He was worrying about the team! It wasn't going to do anybody any good to have him worrying. And all I said was we could handle it."

"We!" He pounced on the word like the panther he sometimes seemed. "And since none of the rest of you know a damn thing about it, who do you suppose that leaves?"

"No one is forcing you," she said evenly. "Don't do it. You're very good at saying no, as I recall. In fact, I can personally attest to it." The words were out of her mouth before she even knew she was going to say them.

Dear God, shut me up! she thought as she clutched Duncan close and Joaquin stalked across the shop to loom over her, chest heaving, nostrils flaring, a muscle ticking violently in his temple.

"You think walking out was easy?" he snarled. "You think I didn't want what was on offer?"

She winced at his flippant "on offer" comment, but then drew herself together and met him toe-to-toe. "I'd say it was pretty obvious you didn't. What was it you said? Oh yes. 'You can't just cold-bloodedly make a man want you.'" She quoted him verbatim. The words were burnt on her brain. "And it was true. You didn't want me."

"The hell I didn't!" he shouted.

Duncan's face crumpled. He waved his fists and started to cry.

"Now look what you've done!" Molly turned away, shushing the baby, all the while her mind spinning over Joaquin's furious claim "the hell I didn't!"

So he *had* wanted her?

She'd thought he was telling her off, refusing what was distasteful to him.

But if he wasn't, then why had he refused? She had been, as he'd so crudely put it "on offer" that night. To him, anyway. But he'd turned his back and walked away.

Why?

When Duncan had quieted sufficiently, she turned back to him, demanding, "So tell me, then, why didn't you take me up on my offer? Why didn't you take *me?*" She forced herself to be as blunt as he had been, though her cheeks burned as she said it. "And don't tell me it was some misguided bit of nobility on your part."

"I wouldn't think of telling you any such thing," he said harshly, and abruptly brushed past her, his arm brushing her sleeve, as he stalked toward the door.

"Running again?" she asked his back.

He stopped in his tracks, turned and glared. His jaw bunched. "Lachlan is my friend," he said. "If you need my help—for anything but coaching—ask me."

LACHLAN HAD SURGERY that evening.

He needed two pins in his ankle, a non-weight-bearing cast,

and a battle-ax of a ward nurse to bully him into doing what he was told and into not getting up before he was permitted to, Fiona reported the next morning when Hugh brought her home to check on Duncan and Molly and to pick up a few things she needed.

"He's very cranky," she said. "He hates being laid up. And he's worried about the team. He's especially worried about Tommy."

Tommy, Fiona's nephew, was the one who had been challenging him for the ball. Lachlan hadn't been wearing shin guards and Tommy had kicked him.

"It's not Tommy's fault," Molly said. "We've all told him that."

"I know. And I called him from the hospital after Lach's surgery to tell him everything was okay. But he's still upset. And Lachlan's worried about him. And a thousand other things. He's given me a list of things that need to be done. Things to practice." She gave a long-suffering sigh as she pulled it out of her pocket.

"Give it here." Molly took it and tucked it in hers.

"You'll give it to Joaquin."

"I'll see it gets taken care of. Don't worry. And tell Lachlan not to worry. His job is to get better. When can he come home?"

"*If* he behaves and does everything he's supposed to do and nothing he isn't—" Fiona rolled her eyes at the likelihood of that "—he'll get to come home on Sunday."

"Not in time for the tournament, then."

"No. But Joaquin can manage."

"Yes." Molly agreed. Which meant yes, he could. It didn't mean yes, he was going to. The Pelican Cay Soccer Tournament looked to be all hers. She packed a diaper bag with all Duncan's stuff in it, took a couple of bottles of the breast milk Fiona had stored in the freezer, put them in a thermal sack, plopped Duncan into his baby backpack and headed for the door.

"You don't have to take him with you," Fiona protested. "I can take him with me when I go back to Nassau this afternoon."

Molly shook her head. "We'll be fine. You don't need more distractions." She hoisted the backpack—and baby—onto her shoulders.

"If you're sure…" Fiona said. "It would be easier."

Molly grinned. "I'm sure. Go take care of the big baby and leave the little one to me."

GUESTS WERE STRAGGLING down to breakfast at the Moonstone when she and Duncan got there. At the sight of them, Suzette came hurrying out of her office.

"How is he? Have you talked to him?"

"No, but Fiona just came home. He's okay. Had surgery last night. Might get home by Sunday. He's only fretting about the soccer."

"Soccer doesn't matter," Suzette said.

Molly shrugged. "It does to him. Gotta run. I'm going to be late for practice." She sprinted up the stairs and banged on Joaquin's door.

It was a minute—and a few more loud bangs—before she heard movement. And grumbling. But at last the door opened.

Joaquin stood there bare-chested, clad only in a pair of shorts, his hair rumpled, his cheeks unshaven. His scowl deepened when he saw her. "I'm not coaching."

Molly shrugged. "Your choice." She pushed past him into the room, dropped the diaper bag on the bed and shifted her way out of the backpack, then plucked Duncan out of it and thrust him into Joaquin's unsuspecting arms.

"Hey! What are you doing?"

"You said to call if I needed help. I do. Key to the house is in the backpack. There're bottles in the bag and clean diapers." She waggled her fingers at him as she went out the door. "Have fun."

HE DAMNED WELL wasn't going to go running after her!

But he kicked the door shut after she'd gone—loud enough that he was sure she could hear it on the front porch—and then he stood there staring at the baby, wide-eyed and bewildered, in his arms.

"What am I going to do with you?"

Duncan blinked guilelessly at him and waved his arms around with exactly the sort of vague aimlessness Joaquin felt.

"Sit here." He plunked the baby on the bed so he could at least get dressed.

But Duncan wobbled, tilted, then toppled over.

Joaquin rubbed a hand down across his face. Jesus. What did you do with a kid who couldn't even sit?

Well, you didn't shave. And you didn't take a shower, that was for sure.

He wedged the baby between the pillows, grabbed shorts and a T-shirt and yanked them on as quickly as he could, watching Duncan like a hawk the whole time lest the baby squirm off the bed.

But Duncan wasn't interested in squirming. He contented himself grabbing the pillowcase and sucking on it. Did that mean he was hungry? Had the kid eaten?

He couldn't exactly ask. But he did anyway.

"Want breakfast?"

Duncan grinned. Whatever that meant.

On the off chance that Duncan was hungry, he found one of the bottles Molly had put in the bag. He sat on the bed and picked Duncan up, cradling the boy in his arms and poking the bottle in the direction of his mouth.

Duncan gurgled and batted it away.

"Not hungry, then?" He tried again just to be sure. But Duncan wasn't interested. He watched Joaquin carefully, his lower lip jutting every time Joaquin started to move away.

Damn Molly McGillivray anyway! How could she do this to him?

"So," he said to the baby. "What do you want to do? Go to the beach? Take a swim? Pick up girls?"

Duncan looked interested in all three possibilities. He gurgled and waved his arms.

"Okay. Let's go." Joaquin stuffed his feet into a pair of thongs and combed his hair with his fingers. Then he picked Duncan up, plopped him in the backpack and wriggled it onto his shoulders—a feat of balance and dexterity he'd never entirely appreciated when he'd seen Lachlan do it. He appreciated it now. Then together they went downstairs.

Every woman in the lobby made a beeline for them.

"Oooooh, isn't he precious?"

"Oh, he's darling."

"Ah, he's gorgeous. Look at that smile."

They crowded around twittering and fluttering, making silly noises and chucking Duncan under the chin. Every one of them offered to give Joaquin a hand. If he'd been looking for a way to draw female attention, obviously carrying a baby around was the way to do it. If he'd wanted to foist his charge off on someone else for the morning, he'd have had no trouble at all.

But he didn't. He was determined to prove he could do it on his own. Molly had obviously thought she could back him into a corner and force him to coach by sticking him with the baby instead.

Well, he'd show her.

It was not exactly a walk in the park. Or a day at the beach. Not the sort he was used to anyway. He took Duncan down to the sand where he spread out a towel on the sand, then he handed Duncan a rubber duck Molly had tucked in the bag. While the baby gummed it to death, Joaquin slathered him with sunscreen.

Then Duncan rolled in the sand.

Joaquin groaned. He picked the boy up and carried him into the water. Duncan was delighted. He wriggled. He bounced. He was as slippery as a fish. It took all Joaquin's concentration to hang on to him. But it was fun.

The only drawback was that Duncan wasn't much of a conversationalist. It would have been more fun to have Molly there to talk to.

But Molly was at the soccer field.

He refused to think about her. They bobbed around in the waves until Duncan began to fuss.

"What now?" Joaquin asked him. "Tired? Hungry? Bored?"

Duncan rubbed his eyes and cried because the saltwater stung them.

"Oh, hell." What did you do for a baby with stinging eyes? If Molly had been there, she would have known.

But Molly was at the soccer field.

He carried Duncan back up to the towel and sat down with him, knowing enough this time not to plop him down and expect him to sit on his own. The tears solved the problem. The crying stopped. Duncan took a handful of sand and thrust it into his mouth.

"Hey, don't do that!" Joaquin wiped away the sand. Duncan screwed up his face and turned red. "And stop that crying!"

But Duncan wasn't crying. He was filling his diaper.

Where were the bloody women when you needed them?

Well, he knew where Molly was.

She was at the soccer field.

But she would never be able to do with those kids what Lachlan could have done. What *he* could do, if he were there.

But he wasn't there. He was at the beach with Duncan who needed changing and was eating sand again.

"Quit that!" Joaquin snatched the boy up into his arms and headed back to his room. He didn't need an audience for his first fumbling attempts to change a baby.

It was a good thing Duncan was patient, he thought. But

even after he'd got the baby changed, Duncan was still sandy and sticky from the sea water.

In the end, because he didn't know what else to do, he stripped them both and took Duncan into the shower with him. By the time they were clean and dry and dressed again, Joaquin felt as if he'd climbed the child-care equivalent of Mount Everest.

Take that, Molly McGillivray, he thought grimly.

But Molly didn't know.

She was still at the soccer field.

UNTIL THIS MORNING Molly had always thought she was in pretty good shape. She ran, she lifted weights. She did a certain number of crunches. But running with a bunch of twelve- to fifteen-year-old boys had a way of making a thirty-one-year-old woman face reality.

Reality was that she was going to die before noon.

They drilled and they ran, and they kicked and they ran, and they dribbled and they ran. And Molly tried gamely to keep up with them.

As Lachlan's sister she had spent more of her childhood than she wanted to remember trying to kick balls past him into a makeshift goal. She knew all about the value of repetition. So she did it with them—again and again and again—until her lungs screamed for air and her legs felt like rubber.

"*¿Estés loca?*" a rough masculine voice demanded from directly behind her. "Sit down before you collapse." A hand came to rest on her shoulder, and Joaquin gave her a none-too-gentle push downward.

Powerless to resist, she sat. Duncan, with his bottle, was thrust into her arms. "Feed him, I will deal with this."

Putting his fingers to his mouth Joaquin gave a short ear-splitting whistle that stopped everyone in their tracks. "Come here! Now! We have work to do."

It was a whole different world.

While Molly had been their "coach," they had argued and

bickered and fussed that she wasn't doing it the way Lachlan had done it. She doubted if Joaquin was doing everything the way Lachlan did it. But they didn't say a word because Joaquin knew what he was doing. They were responding to authority.

She'd been a cheerleader.

Joaquin was a leader, period.

He kicked the ball, bounced it off his head, his chest, his thighs, his shins, his feet and ankles, all the while talking intently to the boys, making it look effortless. He played soccer the way Lachlan did, the way Hugh flew and Fiona sculpted and Syd ran the world. With awe-inspiring competence.

Molly couldn't help but watch—and admire.

And why not? He was beautiful. There was no denying that. His movements were quick and graceful. His body hard and strong. It made her shudder even now when she thought about his paralysis. And she worried that he might do something here that would cause him an injury.

But he asked no quarter and gave none. He played with them, tested them, challenged them. All of them, but especially Tommy.

"Life happens," he told Fiona's nephew. "You do what you have to do and you don't look back."

"But—" Tommy was still guilt-ridden.

"Did you do what you were supposed to do?"

The boy nodded.

Joaquin did, too, satisfied. "Then you did right. And Lachlan knows it. Come on. Let's go. You steal it from me."

Of course Tommy couldn't. But he tried gamely and got a grin and a thumbs-up whenever he made a good play. All the kids wanted to please. And when Joaquin finally said they were finished, they groaned and argued, insisting they could keep going.

"No." He shook his head. "You need to take a break."

"But—" they protested.

"No. Go away. Do something else. Forget this. Go swimming. Go fishing. Go do long division."

Moans and groans met that suggestion. Still they didn't leave.

What about this? they asked him. What about that? What should I do if—

Patiently he answered all their questions. Standing there, barely breathing hard, idly tossing the ball back and forth between his hands, he listened and talked and looked totally at home. Totally comfortable. Exactly right.

"You should be a coach," she said when the boys finally left.

He shook his head.

"But you love it."

He shoved dark damp hair off his forehead and wiped a hand over his sweaty face, then he hunkered down next to her. "It's never been that I didn't want to do it, Molly. I've *always* wanted to do it."

"Then why—"

"Because if I play, if I coach, if I do anything with soccer at all, I won't want to do what I have to do. And I have to go home and work with my father. I made a commitment."

"But if you hate it—"

"I gave my word. It is," he explained, "a matter of honor." His mouth twisted and he lifted a sardonic brow. "Perhaps 'misguided,' you would say."

The words were like a knife, and Molly knew she deserved them. She bent her head. "Not misguided," she muttered.

Whether he heard her or not, she didn't know. He stood up, looming above her, blocking the sun.

"I will do the rest of the practices," he said almost formally. "And the games. You will take care of Duncan, yes?"

Molly looked up and met his hooded gaze. "Yes."

"Good." He gave a curt nod and walked away.

CHAPTER SEVEN

HONOR, JOAQUIN THOUGHT, was hell.

It had made him walk away from making love to Molly for the wrong reasons. It required him to step into Lachlan's boots as a soccer coach and made him want again the game he so loved while he knew he had to do the right thing and keep his word to his father.

It also meant honoring his parents by smiling politely when, on Thursday afternoon, his mother offered him to Marianela Delgado. On a plate.

Well, maybe not on a plate.

But that was what it felt like.

She had flung her arms around him as if he'd been missing for years. Had smothered him in kisses, all the while poking him in the ribs and saying he was too thin. Then she'd dragged him across the soccer pitch toward the helicopter to meet her widow friend Esperanza Delgado. And then she'd drawn forward a pretty, petite, dark-haired young woman and placed her hand in his.

"This is Marianela," she said as if she were handing him the key to the universe. And then she turned to the young woman and said fervently, "Marianela. My son." The amount of meaning she got into those two words defied description. But Joaquin knew—as he suspected Marianela did—what she meant.

My son. My pride. My joy. The focus of all my dreams for the future of my family and my happiness.

Marianela smiled shyly and greeted him in Spanish. And

he did likewise, careful to be polite but completely neutral. The slightest interest or enthusiasm would give his mother false hopes.

"I've been telling Marianela all about you," his mother announced with enough enthusiasm for both of them. "All about your soccer playing and your traveling and how that is over now and you are finally settling down...."

She was going to make it difficult, Joaquin could tell. He opened his mouth to tell her bluntly but politely that "settling down" did not mean instant marriage to the woman of her choice, when all at once his mother squealed.

He flinched, startled, and turned to see Molly coming out of Fly Guy's shop toward them with Duncan in her arms. She had kept her part of the bargain, taking care of Duncan last night and today while he'd worked with the soccer team. He'd thought she might come to see how things were going, but he'd never once spotted her.

She'd stayed completely away.

Now she didn't even look his way. She was focused entirely on Fiona. Duncan was, too, bouncing and waving his arms at his mother.

"*Ay, qué bonito! Precioso! Es tuyo?*" his mother asked Fiona.

Fiona beamed. "Yes. This is Duncan." She took him from Molly and gave him a hug and kiss, then held him out to Ana Santiago to do the same.

All attempts to shove him and Marianela together were forgotten as his mother swept the baby into her arms, making silly noises, cooing and gooing.

He had to give Duncan credit. The kid didn't scream or even blink. He simply regarded the crazy lady with stoic amazement as she burbled and babbled at him.

"Such a gorgeous baby," Ana said, finally handing him back to Fiona. "You and Lachlan make beautiful children." She looked over at Joaquin. "My son is handsome, too. I know he will make me beautiful grandchildren."

Joaquin felt blood rise in his face. "Mama!"

One look at Molly told him she was staring from his mother to him in astonishment, and he knew she was just realizing these were his parents.

"I am only saying," his mother went on, undeterred. "And I'm saying, too, that having a beautiful wife will help." Of course her gaze fell on Marianela.

Joaquin's fell on Molly.

The penny had definitely dropped. She was studying the dark, sloe-eyed beauty of his mother's choice, and God only knew what conclusions she was drawing. But Joaquin knew he didn't like them.

"I don't think you have met Lachlan's sister," he said, taking his mother's arm and steering her deliberately in Molly's direction. "This is Molly. Molly, my parents."

To his astonishment, Ana threw her arms around Molly in an *abrazo*. "Ah, yes. Little Molly. Molly the mechanic. *Mira a la mecánica,*" she said to her husband happily. *"Una mecánica hermosa,"* she added, holding Molly at arm's length, studying her and emphatically nodding her approval. "Lachlan never said that. He was always telling us about his little tomboy sister."

"Lachlan," Molly said grimly, "has a big, but selective, mouth."

Both his parents laughed heartily at that, and his father shook her hand saying, "I always thought of you as little. But you are not so little now."

"No, I'm all grown-up," Molly agreed with a smile. "It took a while, but I'm here." She didn't look his way at all, but he knew who the words were meant for.

"Hugh tells us his business would not survive without you," Ana continued, grasping Molly's hands in hers and squeezing them. "I am so happy to meet you."

"And I'm happy to meet you, too," Molly said politely. "Joaquin has told me about you."

"Does he tell you I am an interfering bossy mother?" Ana

beamed. "Of course he does. And it is true. I *am* an interfering bossy mother. But I only want the best for him."

"Of course you do," Molly agreed politely and her gaze, like his mother's went straight to Marianela.

Joaquin frowned. Enough was enough.

"Come on, Mama," he said, easing her away from Molly before they began conspiring against him. "I'm sure Molly has to get back to work. And it's time we got you all up to Lachlan's house."

"Oh, but—" his mother protested.

But Molly cut in, "He's right. I have a lot of work to do, Señora Santiago. I'm glad I met you, though."

"We will see you again, yes?" his mother demanded.

Molly hesitated. "It's going to be a very hectic few days. I'm sure you'll be very busy. Joaquin will no doubt have lots of plans for you, and I'll have my fiancé staying with me and—"

"He's *staying* with you?" Joaquin demanded, his voice harsh.

Molly squared her shoulders. "That's right."

"Since when?" He heard his parents murmur something to each other behind him but he didn't listen and he didn't care.

"Since he found out there wasn't room at any of the inns." She shrugged. "It doesn't matter. I've got plenty of room at my place." Her tone was even, almost blasé, but he felt as if she were throwing the words in his face.

He ground his teeth. Wanted to say a thousand things. Couldn't say any of them. So he jammed his hands into his pockets and glared at her.

She looked back, unimpressed. Then her gaze shifted to his parents. "It was nice to meet you," she told them. "Now I really must get busy. I didn't get a lot done when Duncan was helping me."

Then, with a smile that seemed to include everyone but him, she headed toward the shop.

IT HAD BEEN a long day.

A hard day.

No longer and harder than any other day she'd had recently, Molly thought—until she'd taken Duncan to the helicopter to meet his mother and instead met the woman who was going to marry Joaquin Santiago.

That had been a kick in the gut.

He might not realize it yet. He might even rail against it. But, she thought wryly, when it came down to the bottom line, he always did the right thing.

And it didn't take a pair of bifocals to see what the right thing was in this case. His mother was absolutely right—he and Marianela would make spectacular babies. With her long black hair, slender but curvy body and big brown eyes, Marianela would definitely be an asset in the "beautiful grandchildren" sweepstakes. It wasn't hard to imagine the gorgeous black-haired, dark-eyed children she and Joaquin would have.

She'd certainly seemed quiet and sweet. Biddable, Molly supposed, would be the right term.

And if she wasn't exactly the sort of woman a bossy arrogant know-it-all like Joaquin Santiago needed—what he needed, Molly thought, was a lion tamer with a whip and a chair—she would probably be exactly the type of woman he would be happy with.

Once his mother convinced him, at least.

She would. Molly had no doubt about that.

"And more power to her," she muttered grumpily. It would be nice to have that sort of power. It would be nice to have any sort of power at all.

She felt irritable and out of sorts. She needed to get the house cleaned up and the spare bedroom prepared for Carson, and she was tired and cranky and hadn't eaten anything all day. She opened a can of spaghetti and dumped it in a pan, but she didn't feel like eating.

She felt oddly like crying. But after her last furious bout of tears when Joaquin had done the honorable thing by turning his back on her, she had vowed never to cry again. So she wouldn't cry, damn it. She wouldn't.

Irritably she stirred the spaghetti. When it began to burn the bottom of the pan, she dumped it on a plate, poured herself a very big glass of wine and sat scowling at the spaghetti while she drank the wine.

Maybe she should get a cat.

If she had a cat, she could talk to it. Tell it all about the injustices in the world. Scratch its ears. Give it bits of her spaghetti. Well, maybe not. But getting a cat might not be a bad idea. She took a gulp of wine.

Maybe Fiona would lend her Sparks.

A sudden sharp rapping at the front door made her hand jerk, and she spilled wine down the front of her shirt. "Hell."

And with her luck it would be Carson, come even earlier than she'd hoped. Only, instead of finding a seductive femme fatale waiting for him, he'd get a grumpy wine-soaked sun-burned witch.

"Hell again." Molly raked her fingers through her hair and hoped it looked even halfway as good as it did when she actually ran a brush through it. Then she bit her lips to put a little color in them, pasted on her best oh-God-am-I-glad-to-see-you smile, and opened the front door.

Joaquin stood on the porch.

"What do you want?" she demanded. She glared at him, then scowled even more fiercely when she spotted the pair of duffel bags he carried.

"Running away again?" she asked snidely.

"No," he said, striding past her into the living room and dropping his bags on the floor. "Moving in."

Molly spun around and slammed the door, her back hard against it. "What do you mean, *moving in?*"

"Just what I said." He kicked one of the bags with his toe. "You've got 'plenty of room.'" He quoted this afternoon's words back to her.

Her eyes narrowed. "Why? Because of Marianela?"

"No!" The word snapped out. But then he scowled and raked a hand through his hair. "Maybe," he allowed. "A little."

"A *little?*" she scoffed.

His jaw tightened. "A little," he said stonily. "It will slow my mother down a bit. That's all." He paused, then met her gaze. "Mostly it's about you and Carter."

"Carson!" She practically shouted it. "His name is Carson!"

Joaquin brushed it off. "Whatever. I gave up my room at the Moonstone. They'll give it to him. He can stay there."

Molly couldn't believe it. "It might have escaped your notice," she said through her teeth, "but I have a far better chance of seducing him if he's here."

"You don't want to make it easy for him."

"I don't?"

"No. You want to make it difficult for him."

"I do? Why?" She felt like Alice, fallen down the rabbit hole. Joaquin was speaking her language. She understood all the words. But nothing made sense.

"He needs to want you," Joaquin told her. "But you can't just make it easy for him—"

"Heaven forbid," Molly said, really annoyed now. "We all know how successful that is," she added with bitter irony.

Joaquin's eyes flashed dark fire. "We've already talked about that. We're talking about this now. If he stays here, it will be too easy for him. You've got to put obstacles in his path."

"I don't think he needs obstacles in his path," Molly said drily. It seemed far more likely to her that, faced with any sort of obstacle, Carson was likely to shrug and take the path of least resistance.

But Joaquin disagreed. "Of course he does. A man doesn't value what he doesn't have to work for."

"And you think he'll work to go to bed with me?"

Her question seemed to pull him up short. For a moment

he didn't reply at all. His mouth opened, but no sound came out.

"Odd that you should keep having these stunned reactions to the very notion of going to bed with me," Molly said shortly.

Joaquin's teeth came together with a snap. "Do you still think I don't desire you?" he demanded.

"It doesn't matter whether you do or not," Molly said with painful honesty. "We both know you're not going to do anything about it."

At her words, something in Joaquin seemed to snap. He grabbed her and kissed her with such heat and such fury that she thought they might go up in flames right where they stood. She didn't care. It didn't matter. Nothing mattered but this. But him!

His hands slid under her T-shirt, stroking her breasts through the lace of her bra, then unfastening it to caress her bare skin. She trembled and felt him tremble, too. He tugged up her shirt and he bent his head, kissing her breasts, stroking them with his thumbs, pebbling her nipples.

She shuddered. Her own hands gripped his shirtfront, clawed, petted, stroked. She needed—she *wanted*—

—the damn phone to stop ringing.

"Don't answer it," Joaquin muttered, his mouth against her breasts. "Don't move."

But she had to. "It might be Fiona. She might need help. Or…or Carson."

Oh, God. Carson.

"I have to get that," she insisted, and trying to pull her wits together, went to answer the phone.

It was Syd, full of news and plans for the festival. Was the banner Molly had been working on finished? No. Well, that was all right. It didn't matter. Syd knew how busy she had been taking care of Duncan and all. But now that Duncan was back with Fiona and she had time could she help out with the art show? And would she do some face painting one afternoon at the carnival? And wasn't it wonderful that things were coming along so well despite Lachlan's accident?

"Yes," Molly said tonelessly. "Yes." And "Yes," again.

She'd do anything. Everything. If only she didn't have to turn around and face what she'd almost done with the man standing in her living room.

"Terrific," Syd said happily. "You're a pal! One of the good 'uns, Mol'."

"Oh, definitely," Molly said.

It didn't matter if Syd heard the irony in her voice. Molly knew it was there. That was enough.

She hung up and turned to find Joaquin standing in the doorway behind her. "I shouldn't have done that," he said.

"No."

His face looked strained, harsh. No devil-may-care man this, she thought, but didn't take the time to wonder why. She knew why. Things were getting complicated. Demanding. And where women were concerned Joaquin didn't do complicated or demanding.

He just did honorable, she thought with bitter humor.

"I still think it would be a good idea if I stayed," he said. She stared at him.

"I do," he insisted. "You want to wake Carson—" for the first time he came down on her fiancé's correct name with both feet "—up. You can do that by not being as available as he expects you to be. His interest will be provoked. He'll take a second, harder look—and see that you're not just his old pal Molly but a delectable desirable woman."

"Whereupon I invite him home to go to bed, to make love, and you're in the room across the hall?" she finished for him.

His mouth twisted. "I didn't say I had it all worked out. I said it was a good idea if I move in, that it would provoke him. Maybe he can invite you back to the inn. No," he corrected himself almost once, "that's not a good idea."

"Why not?"

"Lachlan."

"Lachlan isn't even here. He won't be back until Sunday."

"Even so," Joaquin muttered. Brown eyes met hers. "Don't worry. We can improvise."

"Is that what we were doing in the other room?" she asked. If he wasn't going to talk about it, she was.

He rubbed a hand over his face. "We were making a mistake," he said.

"Again."

His teeth set. "If you like."

"And we won't make any more of them." It wasn't a question. It couldn't be a question. She couldn't take the uncertainty any longer.

He ran his tongue over his lips, but he met her gaze steadily. "Whatever you want, Molly."

"I don't want you to kiss me again."

His expression became shuttered. He let out a slow careful breath. "If that's what you want."

"It is, damn it."

He nodded slowly, then turned away. "I'll put my gear upstairs."

HE LAY ON THE BED and stared at the ceiling. Overhead a fan circled lazily. In the corner on the floor his bags lay open. His clothes and papers were scattered on the chair and the bureau, staking his claim the way he would claim his turf in a match.

This field is mine, he would say by his presence, his actions, his domination.

It felt exactly the same here.

Something else felt familiar as well. It didn't happen often, thank God, but it wasn't unheard of to feel out of sync, to lose the rhythm, the sense of inevitability, of movement, of flow.

Then all you could do was try to find it, to run desperately, frantically, urgently. Like he was doing now.

The news that Carson was going to be staying with Molly

had sent a stab of panic straight through him. It was wrong; he was convinced of that. It wouldn't prove anything, except that Sawyer was as susceptible to temptation as the next man.

He would bed her. He might even marry her.

But would he love her?

As far as Joaquin was concerned, Carson had to prove it.

And if he did? If he loved Molly the way she deserved to be loved and demonstrated it?

He shoved the thought away. He'd never let himself think about losing.

He damned well wasn't going to think about that!

CHAPTER EIGHT

SOMETIMES, MOLLY THOUGHT, life was bizarre beyond words.

Here she was, plotting to seduce her own fiancé, and at the same time allowing another man to move into her house.

And not just any man, either.

A stud. A heartthrob. The Casanova of the pitch. A man who could take his pick of almost all the women in the Western world. And quite frequently did.

Carson would be appalled.

If Carson even noticed.

Despite Joaquin's insistence that he would, Molly wasn't sure. Carson's mind was generally on far more compelling things than who was sleeping in his fiancée's spare bedroom. And she didn't imagine for a minute that he would believe there was anything more risqué going on than that.

He probably didn't even believe she could kiss the way she did.

Until a few days ago, she wouldn't have believed it, either. And apparently it hadn't been a one-off. She was still feeling a little shattered from this afternoon's encounter. If Syd hadn't rung when she had—

Molly pressed her fingers to her eyes. It didn't bear thinking about!

The trouble was, of course, thinking about it was all she'd done since. That and keep out of Joaquin's way for fear of doing it again!

Fortunately he had taken her at her word. She'd stayed

downstairs and he'd gone up. She'd fixed a meal in the kitchen, though she hadn't been able to swallow a morsel. And she didn't invite him to share with her. She remembered the last meal they had shared all too well.

It didn't matter anyway. He came downstairs while she was in the kitchen, and from the stony look on his face, she imagined he remembered, too. Quickly she'd turned her back, and he'd gone out without a word.

When she heard the door shut, she peeked out past the kitchen curtains to watch him leave, wondering if perhaps he had changed his mind about staying after all. But she hadn't seen him carrying any duffel bags. When she was sure he was out the gate and far away, though, she darted upstairs to be certain.

His duffels were still there. The sheets she'd set on the bed this morning, intending to make it up when she had given Duncan back to Fiona, had already been put on the bed.

His shaving kit was in the bathroom. There was a folder full of papers on the bureau and his clothes were tossed carelessly on the chair.

So apparently he had no intention of leaving. On the contrary, it looked as if he were settling in.

Or maybe it was part of the plan he'd outlined for her earlier—about letting himself be an "obstacle" for Carson to overcome.

It was all too convoluted for her.

She should never have started this. It had seemed so simple, so sensible when she'd thought of it. Like preventive maintenance on one of the mokes or the Jeep. Her relationship with Carson had been dodgy, like an engine needing its timing fixed, its spark plugs gapped.

So she figured she'd give it a tune-up, get it running more smoothly, get better mileage.

God, what a fool she was.

And what was even more difficult was that Carson had no idea. He would come home this weekend and expect everything to be exactly the way it had always been, with no notion that she'd been messing around under the hood, as it were, while he was gone.

When he'd left they'd had a serviceable if not terribly exciting engagement.

And now they had—what?

She didn't even know anymore.

For a woman who liked things clear and uncomplicated, she was in decidedly murky waters. And it was all her own fault.

She really did need a cat. Cats had a way of keeping you in line, reminding you what was important—like food and naps. They didn't tinker with spark plugs. Or engagements.

Speaking of which, she wondered how long it would be until Joaquin was engaged himself.

That was probably where he'd gone tonight—off to spend the evening with his parents and the prospective bride.

She felt an odd hollow ache when she thought about it. Stupid, really. It wasn't as if she had any claim on him. It was just that she hadn't thought anyone else would, either. He'd always made it clear that he wasn't the marrying kind.

But then so had her brothers. Lachlan, especially, had never given any indication that he wanted to settle down until somehow Fiona blind-sided him. Then he'd practically moved heaven and earth to get her to say yes.

Rakes make the best husbands. Wasn't that some sort of axiom? Or old wives' tale?

In Lachlan's case it was certainly true. A more devoted husband—and father—would be hard to find. And Hugh, too, who'd sowed some wild oats of his own after Carin Campbell had married Nathan Wolfe, had, once he'd found Syd, become as domestic as a cat.

Would Joaquin?

Molly stared out the window into the darkness and felt a hard lump in her throat. Her fingers knotted together fretfully. "What do you care?" she asked herself angrily.

And she answered out loud, "I don't!"

Which meant she had better get a cat sooner rather than later as she was already starting to talk to herself.

She went to bed at midnight. Joaquin hadn't come back. There were revelers in the streets already. The earliest arrivals coming for the festival and for homecoming activities had begun to assemble today. She could hear noise and music from the Grouper three streets away.

Had Joaquin taken Marianela there to show her a little bit of the island "culture"? Or were they with Fiona and the Santiagos, sitting on the deck overlooking the beach, enjoying quiet conversation? Or had he taken her off on a walk along the beach so he could have her to himself?

Was he kissing Marianela now the way he had kissed her only hours ago?

"Hell." Could she think of nothing else?

She turned off the light and went to bed. She didn't sleep. That would have been too much to expect. The steel drums from the Grouper kept up a steady beat in the background. Nearer at hand, sounds of frogs croaking in the garden kept her awake. A breeze came up, clattering through the palms. Now and then there was a whoop and holler of a reveler with a few too many beers and way too much enthusiasm. Twelve-thirty became one. One became two. She heard more people in the street, heading home from the bars. Snatches of laughter, the refrain of a song.

Then nothing.

All was quiet. The wind died down. There was only the distant sound of the surf.

The island had gone to sleep. Everyone except her.

And Joaquin.

He wasn't asleep. Not across the hall anyway. He might be in bed, though. He probably *was* in bed—in Marianela's arms.

He wouldn't come back tonight at all. She knew that. It didn't matter that his duffel bags were here. It didn't matter that his clothes were strewn everywhere. They weren't what mattered.

Molly knew what mattered to Joaquin—and it wasn't the stuff he'd left across the hall in her spare room.

She rolled over and hugged her pillow, wallowing in misery, trying to trick herself out of it, trying to pretend it was Carson she held. But her imagination wouldn't let her. It couldn't conjure up Carson. It wasn't Carson who was in her mind tonight. Or in her heart.

And then, she thought, she heard the door.

At least she heard something. A soft creak. She raised up on her elbows and held perfectly still, listening, intent. Doubting her hearing.

But then she heard it again. Yes, it was the creak of hinges. She heard the click as the door shut. The floorboards squeaked. Footsteps crossed the living room and started up the steps.

She eased herself back down onto her side, her eyes open just enough to see him when he turned into the other room.

Instead he stopped in the hall and turned toward hers. Her heart thumped against her chest so loudly she was sure he would hear it across the room. He didn't move, just stood there looking in.

She didn't move. Couldn't if her life had depended on it. She couldn't talk to him tonight. Couldn't smile and ask how his evening went, pretend a cheerful interest in the lovely Marianela. Didn't want to see that he had been kissing her.

Go. Just go. She pleaded silently.

But he didn't. He said her name instead. "Molly?"

She ignored it, tried to breathe as evenly and quietly as she could so he would think she was asleep.

He came closer, all the way to the bed.

She stopped breathing, thinking for sure he would leave.

Instead, he sat down beside her!

Startled, she jerked and rolled to face him. "What are you doing here?" she demanded.

"I figured it was about time you had another lesson." His voice was rough and slightly slurred.

She sat bolt upright. *"What?"*

"Get you ready for Carson Bloody Perfect Sawyer," he said raggedly.

She frowned, and the penny dropped. "You're drunk!"

"Damn right I am." He sounded belligerent. And a little petulant. Like Lachlan had when Fiona had dumped him and wouldn't take his calls.

"Why?" Molly demanded. "Did your girlfriend send you home frustrated?"

"I don't have a girlfriend!"

"That's not the way it looked to me. Marianela—"

"Isn't my girlfriend, damn it! I just met her today!"

"Well, you're a fast worker, Joaquin," she said with false sweetness. "I'm sure it won't take you long."

She tried to push him away or scramble out the other side of the bed, but he had one arm on either side of her and she was trapped. He was so close she could feel the warmth of his breath on her cheek.

"I don't want Marianela," he said through his teeth. "She's my mother's idea of the perfect wife. Not mine. And I don't want to talk about her, either. I want this!"

And he took her mouth with his.

It was not the fierce harsh angry kiss she'd been expecting. It was careful. Controlled. Deliberate.

At first nothing touched but their lips. And they met softly, gently, slowly. They teased. Tasted. Tempted.

Oh, how they tempted.

By not pressing, by holding back and controlling, he made her ache, made her need, made her want to press closer, increase the intimacy, stoke the fire.

He invited her to respond, to deepen, to give and receive, to learn and to explore. He barely *did* anything. He was simply there.

But *there* was what mattered. There on his lips she could

taste the whiskey. There in the softness of his hair, she could breathe in the scent of the sun and the sea. There was all around her something uniquely Joaquin.

So close she could touch it.

Close. But not enough.

He only touched his lips to hers. He didn't thread his fingers through her hair. He didn't grab her and haul her hard against him.

She couldn't help it. She wanted more.

More taste. More scent. More him.

All her good sense fled. All her reasoned arguments vanished.

Carson? She didn't even think of him.

She didn't know which of them deepened the kiss. She had no sense of who moved, who led. But the kiss was no longer quite so gentle, soft, teasing. It was like a fire freshly fed. The need deepened. Desire flooded. Passion demanded more.

And eventually even *more* wasn't enough.

Molly fell back on the bed and Joaquin came with her. Their bodies as well as their mouths crushed together. Hips shifted. Legs tangled. Hands explored.

Some tiny part of her did remember kissing Carson. But this was completely different from the clumsy nose-banging efforts they had engaged in as teenagers. It was more intense and passionate than the kisses she'd exchanged with him since. The last time she'd kissed Carson it had been no more exciting than kissing her brothers.

But this!

This was what she wanted.

But not all she wanted.

The tiny part that remembered Carson, remembered something else, too. It remembered that love was more than a few moments' physical passion. It remembered that she wanted a future as much as she wanted the present.

And she would never have a future with Joaquin.

He didn't want what she wanted. Oh, maybe now he did. They *both* wanted that!

But not tomorrow. Not next year. Not in ten.

He was the wrong man. And that was that.

She turned her head, broke the contact. His lips followed, teased, touched. "Molly?"

Tears leaked from the corners of her eyes as she whispered, "I can't."

Still his lips caressed her cheek, followed the line of her jaw, came back to her mouth to coax.

But she pressed her lips together and shook her head.

He pulled back then, and stared down at her, his face hard in the moonlit shadows. "It feels like yes."

"But you said yourself it was a mistake," she reminded him, and was glad her voice didn't break and that he couldn't see her tears.

"Then," he said.

"And now." She smiled sadly. "Nothing's changed."

HE ARRIVED at Fiona's house just past seven, bleary-eyed, unshaven and with a hangover that pounded like half a dozen steel drums in his head.

Fiona, with Duncan in her arms, blinked sleepily at the sight of him.

"Well, you're up early," she said vaguely disconcerted. "Or late. Your parents thought you'd be here last night. When you didn't show up, your mother was afraid you were avoiding them. Worried you'd taken offence at her bringing you a potential bride."

"I don't need her bringing me brides." But that was the least of his problems this morning.

Fiona yawned until her jaw cracked. "Whatever you say. Lachlan thought she was quite sweet when they came to the hospital to see him. Much too nice for you, in fact, is what he said."

"I'm sure he's right." There was an edge to his voice. He couldn't help it.

"Well, you're in a cheery mood," Fiona said. "You might want to lighten up before the parents get up."

"I'll work on it."

"Do that. Quietly. Come on in. No one's even awake yet."

"I'll wait. If you want, I'll make breakfast."

Anything to justify getting out of Molly's place before she woke up. He had barely slept at all. A very cold middle-of-the-night shower had done little to dampen his ardor, and afterward the thoughts tumbling through his head had made his brain feel like Swiss cheese. He'd finally dozed off for an hour or so. But the crowing of Miss Saffron's rooster ended that.

Just as well. He didn't want a morning-after argument when the night before had been nothing he wanted to remember.

He'd left the house that evening because he couldn't have stayed there another minute without going downstairs and trying to pick up where they'd left off.

She'd said no more kissing, and he'd figured he could respect that. But lying there thinking about her and Carson Sawyer had him wanting to chew the furniture. So he'd left. He'd gone for a walk. A long one. He'd run into Charlotte who had offered to keep him company, but he'd declined. He wouldn't be good company tonight, he'd told her.

It was the same reason he didn't go see his parents even though he was sure they were expecting him.

There were other reasons he didn't go see them, too. He didn't want to spend time with Marianela. He was sure she was a very nice girl, but he wasn't interested in a very nice girl. He was only interested in one girl—and she wasn't interested in him.

But she'd sure as hell kissed him as if she were!

How could she possibly still be considering marrying Carson Sawyer when they could start a forest fire at the touch of their mouths?

The question had had no answer. Or none he'd wanted to hear. But it had kept echoing in his head all evening, so he had done his best to drown it out.

He'd started at the Sand Dollar, and hit the Grouper and the Dive Shack and the Starfish Serenade and a couple of bars that were such holes in the wall that they didn't even have names. He hadn't bothered with beer. He'd gone straight to the hard stuff. It had taken the edge off.

And it had given him the false sense that he would be able to control things with Molly the way he could control a ball. He needed to make her see that there was something between them—something far stronger than whatever existed between her and Carson. And so he had gone to her room.

It had started all right. Gentle. Easy. Deft. He had things moving. Slowly at first, sure. But slow was fine. Slow could even be good. Very good. And then the pace had picked up, the movement quickening. Still going well. And then—

And then—his head began pounding harder than before—and then she shut him down. Kept him out.

No crying, no yelling, no fighting. Just quiet rejection. Not since his teenage years had he felt so desperate, so needy, so wild.

And so lost and alone.

He couldn't deal with it. Couldn't stay by himself and face it. And sure as hell couldn't be there when she got up, to get the morning-after politeness she would use to soften the rejection of the night before.

It was preferable to listen to his father ramble on about the future of the family business and his mother about the future of the family name, than to face what really mattered.

"Make breakfast?" Fiona blinked happily at him now. "That's the best offer I've had all day."

She went off to change and feed Duncan, and Joaquin gulped down a couple of aspirin and, trying hard not to be sick, got out eggs and bacon and cheese and peppers and started to work.

To say his parents were delighted to get up and find him there was an understatement.

His father beamed at the sight of him and began telling him all about the merger he was putting together with his friend in New York. His friend had three sons, he told Joaquin, two of whom were deeply involved in the business.

"Like you," he said cheerfully. "Have you had a chance to read over the material I sent you?"

"I'm working on it," Joaquin said, trying to sound as enthused as the old man.

He didn't have to talk at all when he was dealing with his mother. She did all the talking for both of them.

She came downstairs, spotted him and ran to fling her arms around him. "Ah, you're here! Excellent. I was worried. I thought you were afraid of Marianela."

"I'm *not* afraid of Marianela," Joaquin said in a steely voice.

Ana beamed. "Of course you are not. I was worrying needlessly. You recognize quality when you see it. You always did." She patted his arm. "I was never worried about you with all those—those groupies. I knew you wouldn't get involved. I knew you would wait for the right woman. Did I tell you Marianela has a master's degree in finance? So helpful in the business world."

Joaquin sipped a cup of coffee and blessed the effects of aspirin and tried not to wince as he nodded his head.

His mother went on. And on. Marianela was a wonderful cook. And she loved children. She wanted at least six.

He wondered if she had any idea how much time it took to care for one. After his morning with Duncan he was something of an authority. He didn't say so.

She played the piano and the harp, his mother told him. She did counted cross-stitch and glass-blowing and half a dozen other very admirable things.

Is she good in bed? Joaquin was tempted to ask, just to see the look on his mother's face.

Of course he didn't.

He didn't care. He had no intention of taking Marianela to bed. And he was surprised to find that he was now beyond the age where he needed to shock his mother.

He knew she meant well.

And so he smiled and nodded and when she finally ran down and looked at him hopefully, as if he might pull a ring out of his pocket and offer it on the spot, he only said mildly, "Don't get your hopes up, Mama."

She smiled gamely. "You are here, my son. It's a start."

And she did her best to make it a good one, matchmaking her heart out over the breakfast Joaquin had made, telling Marianela what a wonderful cook he was, and telling Joaquin that Marianela had done a Cordon Bleu course, which meant that they would certainly be well matched.

It was embarrassing. But objecting would have made things worse. So he suffered in silence, and Marianela smiled shyly whenever she looked his way. She spoke to his parents and to Fiona, but she seemed to have nothing much to say to him.

After breakfast his mother suggested that he take Marianela down and show her the beach.

He said, "I've got a better idea. None of you has seen the island. Why don't I borrow Hugh's Jeep and give you a tour."

It wasn't what his mother had in mind because it didn't throw him and Marianela together alone. But apparently she understood that forcing the issue was not going to get her what she wanted. So she agreed.

Fiona took Duncan and went with Hugh in the helicopter to pick up Lachlan who'd been released from the hospital in Nassau. "We'll be back this afternoon," she told him. "And we can all have dinner together."

Anything that would keep him busy sounded good to him.

He spent the morning giving his folks and Esperanza and Marianela the grand tour, taking them from the Mirabelle at one end of the island to the Moonstone at the other. He showed them the beach and the tide pools and where the ship wrecked off the point in 1844 and the damage done by the hurricane in the sixties and the remains of the three-hundred-year-old cannon.

Then he took them into town the long way around so he didn't drive past the cricket and soccer field and Fly Guy. ''You've been there,'' he explained. He drove them down past the city dump and the electric plant instead.

''They're really very interesting,'' he said gravely. ''It's always nice to know about the infrastructure of the community.''

And if his mother looked at him oddly, he pretended not to notice. His father, noting his use of the word *infrastructure,* looked pleased.

He parked on the quay and took them on a walking tour of Pelican Town. They went into Miss Saffron's Straw Shoppe, now run by two of her granddaughters, where they got broad-brimmed sun hats for protection before the day got too warm. Then they stopped at the Pineapple Shoppe. For All Your Fruit and Veg Requirement, said the sign in the window— where he picked up fresh pineapples and mangoes for Fiona for tonight's dinner. They walked past the Winn Pixie Grocery, the school, the gaol and the church that was Protestant at nine o'clock on Sundays and Catholic at eleven.

At the top of the hill he turned and led them down Conch Street and avoided passing Molly's in case she was still at home. Instead he took the long way around to Carin's Cottage even though it gave his mother more time to tell him what a clever seamstress Marianela was. The monologue stopped, though, the minute they stepped through the door of Carin's Cottage.

Ana was enchanted with the paintings, sculptures and toys that Carin sold. She only wanted to look and exclaim. So did Marianela and her mother. Joaquin left them to it, and he and his father went outside to sit in the shade.

Carin herself had commandeered her daughter, Lacey, and Marcus and Trevor, two of the boys from the soccer team, to hang paintings for the outdoor art show all up and down Conch Street that was opening this evening.

"Hey, Joaquin," one of the boys called. "Practice still at two?"

He'd forgotten all about the soccer games. "I don't know."

"Practice?" his father frowned. "You are playing soccer?"

"Coaching," Joaquin corrected. "For the moment. Just filling in for Lachlan," he said. "It's his team. Not mine."

"You gotta come," Trevor insisted. He turned to Martin. "Lachlan's a good coach, but he's a goalkeeper. He knows defense. Joaquin knows how to help us score."

"I did what you showed me yesterday," Marcus's eyes were alight. "I practiced all morning. It works." He sounded almost surprised.

"Of course it works," Joaquin rolled his eyes.

His father's brows lifted. "Joaquin is a good teacher?"

"The best!" Marcus said eagerly. "And you should see him play."

"He has seen me." Once or twice. "This is my father," Joaquin told them.

Both looked at Martin with wide-eyed respect. "Can you play, too?" Marcus asked.

"Did you teach him?" Trevor wanted to know.

Martin shook his head. "I am a businessman."

"That's too bad." Trevor was all sympathy. "But at least you got to watch him play. You can come watch us today."

"He's on vacation," Joaquin said quickly.

But his father interrupted. "I would like to see you practice." He turned to Joaquin. "I would like to see you teach."

Joaquin rubbed a hand against the back of his neck. "Mama might have other plans."

"Then Mama can do them on her own," Martin said simply. "We will be there," he told the boys.

"Fantastic! See you there!" And they ran off to finish helping Lacey with the paintings.

Joaquin turned back to his father. "You don't have to come."

Martin just looked at him. "I want to."

Joaquin couldn't imagine why, unless it was to point out his failings. But there was no discussing it further as the women came out of Carin's Cottage just then. They were all laden down with carrier bags full of purchases.

"Carin has invited us all to lunch with her and her handsome husband," Ana said.

"At the Bakery." Carin followed them out and smiled at Joaquin. "If you have time," she added. "Marianela is a fabric artist, and we've found lots to talk about."

"I thought she was a finance major," Joaquin said to his mother.

His mother huffed a little. "I told you, she has many talents."

And the fact was, for the first time since she'd arrived, Marianela seemed actually interested and animated, rather than merely smiling and dutiful.

"That would be great," Joaquin told Carin. "We'll meet you there."

It was working out almost better than he could hope. The day was filling with distractions, and no one was talking about Molly. The fact that she seemed to be hovering at the back of his every thought was annoying, but he was coping. He didn't know what to do about the unexpected announcement by his father that he would come along to soccer practice. But he hoped the old man would become so interested in conversing with Carin and Nathan that he would forget all about soccer practice.

But after lunch when he got up to go, his father came, too.

Practice was already going on by the time they got there. And naturally the first person Joaquin saw as he came over the rise was Molly. Her red hair glinted in the sunlight as she darted in and out, moving the ball down field, then taking a shot at the goal.

Fiona's nephew, Tommy, who was goalkeeping lunged to stop it, but it sailed past his fingertips into the goal.

"Gooooooalllll!" Molly and her half-dozen "teammates" cheered and danced. And then she looked up, saw him coming. Her smile faded. All animation vanished.

"Nice goal." He did his best to sound hearty, but the words felt stiff and awkward. He couldn't quite meet her eyes.

Molly didn't meet his eyes, either. "I thought you might be busy," she said stiffly, "with your parents here and all."

"I said I'd coach the games," he told her just as stiffly.

Her smile was wooden. "Fine. I'll leave you to it. Nice to see you again, Mr. Santiago," she said to his father. And still without looking at Joaquin, she hurried away.

Joaquin watched her go. Wanted to go after her. Wanted to grab her and stop her. Wanted—

He sucked in a sharp breath.

"¿Qué tienes?" His father looked at him closely. "Is something wrong?"

"No. Everything's fine, Papa." He shut his eyes for a moment, gathered his wits. Then, "Vámonos," he called to the boys and clapped his hands. "Let's go. Shirts and skins." He divided them into two teams. "Come on!"

Half the boys stripped off their shirts. He whistled the start, and Marcus kicked the ball into play. They ran, they dribbled, they passed, they kicked. He watched, shouted directions, encouragement, always aware of his father standing on the sidelines. As impatient as Martin had always been with any sort of game, he couldn't imagine why his father had come. But before he could give it much thought, Marcus's footwork caught his attention and he ran onto the field.

"Wait. Stop, Marcus. Like this." And the instincts and experiences of a lifetime took over. The adrenaline kicked in.

He forgot all about his father. He almost forgot about Molly. Not quite. Even as involved as he was, he noticed that she had not gone into the shop, but was standing by the doorway, watching him.

Somewhere inside him the teenager who wanted the girl to notice him woke up and took charge.

"Here," he directed Marcus. "Try this. You defend," he instructed one of the bigger boys as he dropped the ball, tapped it with his instep, then stutter-stepped and darted quickly around him, then passed the ball to Marcus. "Now, you."

Marcus tried. He was slow. He got faster. Surer. More confident.

And Joaquin played with them, challenging them, exhorting them, encouraging them, aware only of the movement of the game and, in the shadow of the shop, Molly still watching them.

Trevor passed him the ball as he ran. The sun beat on his back, but the breeze cooled the sweat that ran in rivulets down his chest as he dodged first one defender, then faked out another, ran around him and slapped the ball across his body, past Tommy's outstretched arms, right into the far corner of the net.

"Goal!" the boys yelled. "Goal!"

He'd scored plenty of goals in his life in bigger matches, in stadiums with thousands upon thousands of people. This was a pick-up practice game with a bunch of kids. But at that moment it was the sweetest goal he had ever scored.

He looked over to see if Molly had been watching.

She was standing in the doorway of the shop, but she wasn't alone. His father stood next to her, and waved him over.

Joaquin hesitated.

And then Trevor yelled, "Chopper's comin'!"

A thrumming noise made him look up to see the helicopter coming in from above the harbor. It hovered for a moment above the field, then slowly settled onto the grass. Then Hugh cut the engine and the silence was deafening. For a moment no one moved.

Then Marcus shouted, "Lachlan's home," and all the boys ran to greet him.

The door opened, and Hugh hopped out first, then Fiona and Duncan. Lachlan climbed out last, hampered by the cast up to his knee and a pair of crutches he wasn't at ease with yet.

The kids ringed him in respectful silence, as if they were afraid to get close. Then Lachlan said something to them— Joaquin wasn't close enough to hear what—and grinned.

The ice broke and all the boys laughed and crowded around him, every one of them talking at once. Then Trevor pointed in his direction, and all the heads swiveled his way. Lachlan nodded and beckoned.

Joaquin started to walk toward them when he saw someone else framed in the chopper's doorway. He was tall and dark-haired and he paused on the threshold, looking around as if he were searching for something.

And then his gaze stopped.

On Molly.

She stood stock-still, staring, mouth agape. And then she

shut it. For an instant her gaze flickered in Joaquin's direction. Their eyes met.

And then, as he watched, she turned to his father, said a few brief words and left him to take off running across the grass toward Carson Sawyer.

Who else?

It was a hell of a reunion.

Joaquin saw it all: the sudden grin on the man's tanned face, the quick jump onto the grass; the open arms—and then the impact of Molly's body against his.

The two of them pressed together, arms wrapped around each other. The fierce embrace, the hungry kiss.

Oh, yes, the kiss.

The image would be emblazoned on his brain forever—Carson Sawyer and Molly McGillivray liplocked.

Just the way he'd taught her.

CHAPTER NINE

SHE COULD FEEL Carson's shock the instant her lips touched his.

His arms went around her, steadying her, clutching her close, but more to keep her from toppling them both over than for any more romantic reason.

For the moment Molly didn't care.

If it had been the kiss of the century, she would have rejoiced. That it wasn't didn't exactly surprise her.

It was enough that she did it. It told Carson that things were changing, that *she* was changing.

And it told Joaquin—dear God, she *hoped* it told Joaquin!—that she knew what she wanted in life, that she wasn't quite the pitiful idiot he most likely believed she was after she had nearly melted—*twice!*—in his arms.

She hadn't had a chance to tell him herself that morning. He'd been gone when she'd finally dragged herself out of bed. She hadn't fallen asleep till nearly dawn. And when she finally did, she'd slept like the dead. She hadn't heard him leave.

She figured he had probably gone to spend time with his parents and Marianela, a supposition confirmed by Fiona when she and Duncan had arrived at the field to meet Hugh who was taking them to Nassau to get Lachlan.

"He was on my doorstep before any of us were up," Fiona had reported, somewhat amazed. "He says he's not interested in Mama's prospective bride, but what else could he possibly be doing there?"

Getting away from me hadn't seemed like a very useful answer. And it was probably too self-centered to be true, anyway. The fact was, Fiona was most likely right. For all that he might not think he was interested in Marianela, he was going home to Barcelona. He was going into business with his father. How long would he be able to pretend that marrying a woman his mother approved of wasn't also part of the Joaquin Santiago Life Plan?

She hadn't said anything, though. But later that morning, when she'd caught a glimpse of him driving everyone around in Hugh's Jeep, she'd been increasingly sure her speculation was true. It hurt a little, but she refused to think about it other than to tell herself it was a good thing in the long run—and the fact that he was occupied with his parents and the prospective bride for the moment meant she wasn't likely to run into him.

She'd been surprised to see him show up at practice. And she hadn't met his eyes when they'd spoken. But that hadn't stopped her looking at his lips.

She'd been kissed senseless by those lips. And dear God, she hadn't been able to stop the wish that he'd do it again. The thought had sent such a shaft of panic right through her that she'd very nearly bolted past him to get back to the shop.

But having run away, she hadn't gone in. It was hot inside, she'd rationalized. There was work she could do on one of the mokes. And so she had lingered in the yard, tinkering with the moke's engine while, in fact, most of her attention had been on the man playing soccer fifty yards away.

And then his father had come over and begun talking.

He didn't know much about soccer, he told her candidly. He had never been much interested in games. But Joaquin, he said, had always been passionate, determined, driven.

"He loves it," Molly said in case his father hadn't noticed. If Joaquin couldn't say that much to his father, the least she could do was say it for him.

Martin had nodded silently, and they'd stood together

watching as Joaquin patiently instructed the boys. There was an enthusiasm and a quiet authority in his words and actions. The boys understood and responded to it. You only had to watch to see how involved he was. And his intensity was contagious. The boys who had gone through the motions while working with her were passionate for him.

And then he'd put it to work in a game, taking a tap from Marcus to move the ball deftly down the length of the field, all of the opposing team incapable of stopping him. The fluid grace of his movements made it all look effortless.

"He is beautiful," Martin murmured, sounding surprised.

Oh, yes, he was that. She nodded, her throat so tight she was unable to speak.

"And a good son," he went on after a moment. "He is coming home to work with me."

Molly nodded. "Yes, he said."

"I was afraid he wouldn't want to," he confided, his eyes still on his son. "He was never interested in the business when he was younger. And it seemed wrong to force him. It was important to let him play. So he could be happy with his choice."

"Yes." It was obvious, however much Joaquin felt that his father didn't understand what drove him, that the older man loved him deeply and wanted him to be happy. But for Molly, being the recipient of Martin's confidences was unnerving.

It made her feel as if Martin believed she knew Joaquin better than she did.

But on reflection she realized she did know him. She knew what he loved, what drove him, what satisfied him, what made him happy.

She even knew the taste of his passion.

She just wasn't supposed to, she thought guiltily.

It had been an enormous relief that Hugh's helicopter had appeared just then, and the increasingly loud thrum of the chopper's engine cut off all possibility of further conversation.

Best of all, though, had been the unexpected sight of Carson. He hadn't come with Dena Wilson after all. Instead he'd stood in the chopper scanning the field, looking for her, then finding her. His eyes had lit up.

Molly's breath had caught.

"Please excuse me," she'd said to Martin. And with one quick glance at Joaquin whose expression told her he knew exactly who that was, she ran.

Away from feelings she should never have had. Away from the man who made her feel them.

But *toward* something, too. Toward her fiancé. To show Carson that she loved him. To prove to herself—and to him— that now was the time to take their relationship to another level. To find passion with the right man.

And to show the wrong one that she could do it.

Carson staggered under the impact, catching her, holding her.

"Hey, Mol'! What's this?" He was grinning until her lips touched his. She smothered everything else with a kiss like no other she and Carson had ever shared.

It was deep, intense, and, on Molly's part at least, determinedly passionate.

So what if they were in the middle of a helicopter landing pad with half the island's teenage boys looking on? Maybe they would learn something.

She was. She was learning that kissing Carson was nothing like kissing Joaquin. Carson's kiss was warm and pleasant and lovely, and his arms were comfortable, familiar and strong as he held her close.

But there was no zing. No sizzle. No passion. No "give me more."

Not yet.

But it was early days, she reminded herself as she pulled back. Carson had no idea how she was feeling, what she wanted. Right now, in fact, he was looking at her a little dazed, a bemused and slightly bewildered smile on his face.

"Wow," he said, the smile turning into a lopsided grin. "I guess I should come back more often."

Molly put an arm around his waist. "Or not leave."

His brows lifted. "Not leave? Hard to run everything from here, Mol'," he said almost apologetically.

"I know. I do. Really." There would be time enough to discuss things like that later. She raised up and kissed his cheek. "I've missed you. I'm just glad you're home."

"Yeah, me, too. We've—" he raked a hand through his hair "—got a lot of catching up to do. Things to talk about."

Molly nodded, relieved that he'd come to the same conclusions. "Absolutely. Let's go."

"Wait. Before you two run off," Fiona hurried over to them. "I wanted to invite you over tonight. Since Lachlan isn't going to any of the homecoming stuff—"

"Except the soccer tournament," her husband interrupted.

Fiona rolled her eyes. "Except the soccer tournament," she echoed drily, "we thought it would be nice to have an open house at our place so all the homecoming islanders can drop by to see him. That means you." She poked Carson in the chest.

He nodded agreeably. "Sure. All right with you, Mol'?"

It would probably mean seeing Joaquin. He would be there with his parents and Marianela. But so what? Molly thought. She couldn't avoid seeing him forever. She didn't *want* to avoid seeing him. She wanted to continue to be friends. Didn't she? "Sure." She mustered her enthusiasm. "We'll bring some food."

"And beer," Carson promised.

Lachlan gave him a grin and a thumbs-up.

"Where you staying?" Hugh asked as he tossed luggage in the Jeep. "I'll run your bags by."

"He's at the Moonstone," Molly said before Carson could answer. He raised his brows in query and she explained, "They had a last-minute cancellation, and I know you like being on the beach more than the harbor side."

Carson nodded, obviously pleased. "Thanks. Sounds good." He turned to Lachlan. "You need help getting to your place?"

Lachlan leaned on the crutches, looking tired but glad to be home and shook his head. "I'll manage." He jerked his head toward the pitch where the boys had returned to practice with Joaquin who had his full attention on them.

"You get him to do that?" he asked his sister, wonder in his voice.

Molly shook her head.

Lachlan smiled. "Might've been worth breaking my leg for." He waved a crutch and wobbled precariously. "Come on, you lot!" he yelled at the boys. "Let's see how good a teacher Santiago is."

HE DIDN'T watch her leave.

He had more important things to think about. Nothing in Joaquin's life had ever been more important than soccer.

Until today.

Today he couldn't keep his mind on anything.

No, not true.

He couldn't keep his mind on the game. He had no trouble at all keeping his mind on Molly, on wondering how she was doing with Carson, wondering *what* she was doing with Carson.

From the looks of their kiss, Joaquin reflected grimly, she would have him dragging her to the altar by nightfall, desperate to get her to bed. Visions of Molly in bed punched him in the gut. The memory of her in his arms taunted and tormented.

"Ooof." The ball hit him in the head.

"Hey!" Lachlan's voice broke in. "*¿Qué pasa, amigo?* What's up?"

"Sorry! Just…distracted…" Joaquin gave his head a quick shake and tried to focus. But he was out of sync, a step late.

For the first time in his life he was glad when Lachlan called things to a halt.

"Go home. Get lots of rest. Be here bright and early," Lachlan told the team as they gathered around him. He consulted his schedule. "First game is at nine. We play at ten. But come early. It never hurts to watch the earlier game. You can learn something every time you watch an opponent," he told them sternly. Then he sent them off and turned to Joaquin. "What the hell is wrong with you?"

"I told you. I was distracted."

"You're never distracted. Unless…" Lachlan eyed him, and Joaquin tried not to fidget under his narrowed gaze. "You worrying about what your old man thinks?"

His old man? Hell, he hadn't given Martin a thought. Now he looked around and spotted Martin standing on the sidelines talking to Carin and Nathan Wolfe.

"Yeah, maybe that's it," he murmured.

"Well, don't let him worry you," Lachlan advised. "Come on. Let's go home. I'm glad to be back, but I need to get off this leg."

There was no possibility of saying he wasn't going to go back to Lachlan and Fiona's tonight. His parents were there. Their friends were there. Everyone he knew on the island would be there.

Undoubtedly Molly and the love of her life would be there.

Unless she'd got him into bed already and they had more interesting things to do, Joaquin thought, his jaw closing with a snap.

He didn't really believe that. Not at first. But as the hours passed and more and more people dropped by to eat and drink and chat—and Molly and Carson weren't among them—he began to wonder.

He helped Hugh, who was grilling steaks and shrimp and local spiny lobsters for the multitudes. He kept track of everyone who came to get a plate of food. No Carson. No Molly.

Finally Hugh decreed that they'd grilled enough, but it was

a good place to stand and keep an eye on things, so Joaquin said he'd just stick around in case anyone came late or wanted seconds. Nathan Wolfe's father and both of his brothers and their wives and children did come late. And while he grilled for them, he watched in vain for Molly.

He spent a while talking to Hugh's father-in-law who seemed pretty much a clone of his own business-obsessed parent. He chatted with the parents of several of the soccer players. He made sure he always had a good view of who came and went.

He never saw Molly and Carson.

"You can stop lurking by the grill now," Fiona said finally. "We've all had more than enough."

"There might be a few stragglers," he suggested.

"I can't think of anyone who isn't here or hasn't been."

"I haven't seen Molly," he said before he could stop himself.

"I imagine she and Carson have a lot of catching up to do."

Which was pretty much what he imagined, too. And he didn't like the idea.

"If you're desperate to be useful," Fiona suggested, "come and help crank the ice cream freezer."

He cranked the freezer. It was on the deck. He could still see the door and the path to the beach. But it was dark now. He wouldn't see them if they came that way. He dished up ice cream.

He consulted his watch and prowled the deck. When Hugh asked sarcastically if he was on sentry duty, Joaquin went into the kitchen and washed dishes, prompting his mother to point out to Marianela how domesticated he was.

At that point he'd had all he could take.

It was after midnight. He left.

It didn't matter where Molly and Carson were. He knew what they were doing. It gave him a pain in the gut.

The Grouper was rocking when he passed. Down near the

dock, the Sand Dollar had a reggae band that he could also hear. A lot of folks out and about, standing in groups, laughing and talking.

He opened the gate at Molly's and stopped, wondering what the hell he'd do if he walked in on them in midseduction. Surely Molly wouldn't bring Carson back here knowing he might walk in at any time.

Or maybe she would. Just to make a point. Show him what a good teacher he'd been. The pain in his gut got worse.

He heard the creak of the porch swing next door and Miss Saffron said, "They ain't home yet."

He didn't know if the breath he let out was a sigh of relief or not.

By one he had nearly paced a rut in the rug.

No Carson. No Molly.

By two he was craning his neck over the gate and looking up and down the road. No Carson. No Molly.

By three he was deep in the bottle of Jack Daniels he'd found in the cabinet, when he heard the murmur of voices outside. Seconds later the latch opened and Molly came in.

"Where the hell have you been?" The words were out before he could stop them. He was scowling like an overbearing father.

Molly, cheeks flushed, hair disheveled, stared at him. Her brows arched. "I beg your pardon?"

He set his whiskey down with a thump. "There's thousands of people milling around. Strangers! Who knows what could have happened!" It was irrational and insane and he knew it.

"Indeed," she murmured. "Who knows?"

He scowled. "We missed you at Lachlan's," he said pointedly.

"We hoped to get there. But Carson spent time with Lachlan and Fiona on the flight from Nassau, so he'd seen them. And he wanted to go see the Cash brothers. Have you met Euclid and Erasmus?"

Joaquin shook his head. "Don't know 'em."

"They're two wonderful old men, but they're kind of shy. They make toys that Carin sells in her shop. But a long time ago, they were fishermen. And when Carson's father died, they came back and fished with Carson. They helped him until he got on his feet. He's never forgotten."

Molly smiled reflectively as she slipped off the shawl she'd wrapped around her shoulders. A serious amount of bare, tanned skin was suddenly on view.

Had Carson kissed it? Deliberately Joaquin looked away, picking up his whiskey glass and taking a swallow. It burned, but not as much as the need to know was burning him.

"So that's where you were? All night?"

She hesitated. "That's where," she said. There was something in her tone that held a suggestion of "want to make something of it?"

He let out his breath slowly. "So how's the seduction coming?" he asked, doing his best to sound casual.

Molly hesitated a second, then toed her sandals off. "It's coming along."

She didn't look at him, just shoved the sandals over next to the door, then yawned and stretched. "It's been a long day," she said, heading for the stairs. "I'm going to turn in."

Joaquin stayed where he was and watched her go, letting his eyes feast on the gentle curves of her body as she climbed the steps. When she'd disappeared into the hall, he lifted his glass and thanked the heavens.

If the seduction was "coming along," she and Carson hadn't made it to bed yet.

As a teacher maybe that made him a failure.

As a man Joaquin was vastly relieved.

SOMETHING WAS DIFFERENT between Carson and her.

Molly lay in bed, staring up into the darkness, and tried to figure it out. But she couldn't put her finger on it, though she tried.

Of course, *she* was behaving differently. She was flirtier, more touchy-feely, more attentive than she usually was when Carson came home.

But Carson was different, too. He had been edgier all evening. Less easygoing. More distracted, as if he had something on his mind. Which was not unusual because Carson always had things on his mind. But this was different. And though he was distracted, he was oddly more watchful, too. Several times she'd caught him studying her when he thought she wasn't looking.

Was it her new haircut? she wondered. Was it her new wardrobe? Was it the way she stayed closer to him when they were out?

How much of his changing could be traced to hers? And how much was he simply changing on his own.

Molly didn't know. And she didn't know how to find out.

It wasn't like fixing an engine, where you could test something, being fairly certain that other things weren't changing while you were doing it.

With people, there were way too many variables.

She wondered if getting him the room at the Moonstone had been a mistake. Would it not have been smarter, regardless of what Joaquin claimed, to have him right across the hall? It certainly hadn't been smart to have Joaquin right across the hall. Not in terms of her peace of mind, at least!

But Carson had seemed pleased. "It will be easier that way."

"Easier?"

"For business. I've got meetings all day tomorrow with the Wilsons. And we're leaving early to look at those condos on Eleuthera. I wouldn't want to disturb you."

She knew he and Tom Wilson from the Lodge were doing some business while he was home, and Carson was never far from his mobile phone and whatever project he was developing. But she'd hoped for a little undivided attention.

It didn't happen.

They'd taken Carson's luggage to the Moonstone, then had

gone downstairs for a drink in the bar, where Carson had run into several old friends back for the homecoming weekend. He and Molly had joined them for a swim and an impromptu volleyball game. Then their "dinner for two" at Beaches turned into "dinner for nine" when they ran into people they knew there, too.

After that he'd suggested they go see Euclid and Erasmus. Molly loved the two old men almost as much as Carson did. And she'd been happy to go see them. Happier, in fact, than if she'd had to watch Joaquin all evening. But it would have been nice to practice a few techniques on Carson.

So far as far as she'd got was his admiring her haircut and one of her new dresses.

She sighed. The seduction was "coming along," as she'd told Joaquin. But it wasn't coming along very fast.

When she'd kissed him good-night tonight, she'd deliberately tried to make it the same sort of kiss Joaquin had given her last night. She started slowly, gently, tenderly, moving her mouth over his. Then she eased closer and, when she felt his lips part, she traced them with her tongue. It felt calculated. Not passionate. It felt studied. Not hungry.

And for the longest time she felt no response. There was no pounding heart against hers. There was no answering pressure.

It was as if he wasn't there.

And then, all at once, he was. Suddenly something in Carson snapped and he took over, deepening the kiss without any help from her. His fingers dove into her hair and he kissed her long and hard and almost, it seemed, desperately.

Startled by his sudden intensity, Molly pulled back and stared into his dark, unreadable gaze.

His lips twisted briefly, then he opened his mouth as if he were going to say something. Say what? She held her breath.

Abruptly he closed his mouth again and, for a second, his eyes, too. He let out a long slow breath and opened them again.

"I'll see you tomorrow." His voice was low and level, with a hint of tautness in it, as if something were being left unsaid.

Molly nodded. "Good night," she'd whispered, and watched him go before she went into the house where, it turned out, Joaquin was waiting to jump down her throat.

"How was her seduction coming?" he'd asked her.

Fine. Maybe.

The question was: Did she want it to?

CHAPTER TEN

SOMEWHERE IN THE MIDDLE of the sleepless night, she faced the answer.

It was no.

She had loved Carson Sawyer for most of her life. In many ways she loved him still. But what they shared was not the sort of love she saw between Lachlan and Fiona or Hugh and Sydney.

She and Carson cared for each other. They had been friends, pals, buddies, mates—whatever you wanted to call it—for years. They'd even done their share of adolescent groping back in the days when they hadn't had their hormones under control. But it had never been very memorable. And they'd tended in recent years to find excuses to do other things when if they'd felt any kind of passion for each other, they'd have been falling over each other in their haste to make love.

They'd never had to fight for control. They'd never had to battle their own inclinations, their own desire.

They'd always found reasons to wait.

And when she had finally found a reason not to wait any longer, it was her wish for a home and family of her own and not her passion for Carson that had prompted her to make a move. She had even doubted that such intense passion even existed.

How about that? Two mistakes for the price of one.

Because, heaven help her, Molly knew now that passion existed. In the past days she had felt herself in the thrall of it, had known its power, its depth, its demand.

She also knew that the man who had inspired it didn't love her. Joaquin Santiago had—at her express request—taught her how to use all her feminine wiles to seduce the man she was engaged to. And instead she had foolishly, stupidly and entirely unwittingly fallen in love with him.

Now what?

In the best of all possible worlds, she would go to Carson tonight and tell him how she felt. He would agree that they were better off as friends than they ever would be married to each other. And then Joaquin would ride in on his white charger and sweep her off her feet, propose to her, and they would live happily ever after.

Well, a girl could dream.

Or she could if she ever managed to fall asleep.

FOR YEARS soccer had been his life. Now at least it was providing him a measure of distraction and a bit of sanity. Without the tournament, Joaquin didn't know how he would have got through the day.

Molly was up and gone before he rose at seven. He had lain awake for hours thinking about her in the room across the hall, feeling a mixture of relief that she was there and annoyance that she wasn't in *his* bed. Finally sometime about dawn he'd fallen asleep from the sheer recent lack of it.

When his alarm went off only a couple of hours later, he'd felt groggy and stupid and out of sorts, which was nothing compared to how out of sorts he felt when he opened the door to see hers wide open and her bed empty and neatly made.

She had gone with Carson already?

The thought had made him slightly sick. *Get over it,* he had told himself sharply. *She's not yours. She never has been. She never will be.*

He had soaked his head under the cold water in the shower, had shuddered madly and felt worse. Then he'd dragged himself off to the pitch to take his mind off her by focusing on soccer.

It worked. It was habit. Muscle memory. Pattern repetition. All of the above. Whatever, the games consumed him. As long as he was focused on the match, he didn't think about what Molly was doing with Carson.

The only time his concentration wavered was in midafternoon just after halftime of the middle game when he thought he spotted her in the crowd. He looked for her again, looked for Carson, too, because seeing them both there would mean they weren't in bed someplace. But he never saw Carson, and he didn't see Molly again.

Maybe he hadn't seen her in the first place. Maybe he'd only wished it.

It was his good luck, he realized later, that by winning, the Pelicans kept having to play more games. They kept him busy all day, playing three by the end of the afternoon. They were completely exhausted, but they were through to the semifinals, having won them all.

"Nine o'clock sharp, be here," Lachlan told them all as they lay on the ground, exhausted. They groaned. But he grinned at them. "You guys were dynamite today."

The groans turned to grins. "We were awesome," Marcus said with considerable satisfaction. "Totally."

"Tomorrow you can say that," Lachlan told him. "If you win. Now go on home and get some rest. Don't party all night."

"No fear," Lorenzo mumbled. "Jus' gonna go home an' catch some zzz's."

The boys and their families and most of the rest of the spectators wandered off. Joaquin studied the throngs of people but he didn't see Molly.

"Lose something?" Lachlan asked him.

Quickly Joaquin shook his head. "No. Just wondering where my folks are. Haven't seen them all day."

"They were here," Lachlan said. "You were too consumed to notice. They left while you were helping Trevor work out his muscle spasm. Said they had a reservation for dinner at Beaches at eight and you can join them there.''

''Thanks.'' He didn't want to go to Beaches. He didn't want to have to sit and make small talk with his parents and Marianela and her mother all the while wondering how successful Molly was being in her seduction of Carson Sawyer.

''Have fun,'' Lachlan said cheerfully. He pushed himself up and leaned on his crutches. ''Don't do anything I wouldn't do,'' he said with a wink.

FORTUNATELY, emulating Lachlan's behavior gave Joaquin a fairly large latitude when it came to deciding how to act. Not that he had any clue how Lachlan would act when it came time to watch Molly get ready to go out for her big formal date with Carson.

She was already home when he got there. He could hear the shower running upstairs. He pretty desperately needed a shower himself. He might not have *played* those three soccer matches today, but he had certainly exerted himself coaching. He was grimy and he was sweaty, and he debated going up and knocking on the door and asking her if she wanted to share.

Dream on, *amigo,* he mocked himself.

Because he couldn't trust himself to do anything else, he stayed resolutely downstairs even after the shower shut off and the door opened and he could hear her footsteps in the hall. His mind's eye had no trouble imagining her wet and in a towel—or less. He shut his eyes and tried to blot it out, but that didn't help.

So he got up and went into the kitchen and got a beer, then banged a few cupboards making himself a sandwich, hoping that doing something would be better than sitting there fantasizing. And it might have been, if he hadn't heard a voice on the stairs a few minutes later.

''Joaquin?'' Molly came halfway down the stairs, barefoot, wearing the dress she called her ''green crayon'' dress. It was every bit as spectacular in its simplicity now as it had been when she'd tried it on in the shop. It made his heart slam just to look at her. "I've got a favor to ask."

"What?" he said warily.

"This dress takes two."

He didn't understand. "Two what?"

"People. One to wear it and one to, um, do the tie gizmos in the back." She turned around.

All he could see was acres and acres of beautiful bare back. His mouth went dry.

"Ah," he said.

"Er," he said.

Dear God, he thought, and prayed for guidance. The tie "gizmos," as she called them, were laces that criss-crossed her bare back and connected with the thin straps that were all that held the dress up. Not only that, they were all the back there was above the bottom of her shoulder blades. Had he noticed that before?

"Could you, um, tie it for me?"

Could he plead ignorance of basic knots? Could he say he was all thumbs? Could he ask her what the hell she was trying to do? Kill him?

He gritted his teeth. "Come here." He set down his beer and wiped his hand on his shorts. "My hand is cold," he warned her.

"Cold hands, warm heart," she quipped, then it seemed as if all her visible skin—and there was plenty—was suffused in a rosy flush. "Never mind," she said quickly. "I'll live. Just do it. Carson's going to be here soon."

"Sure you wouldn't rather wait for *him?*" Joaquin bit out.

She shook her head. "No, thanks. I think he's worried enough about making a good impression tonight. He would want to know I was fully dressed to start out."

Joaquin didn't let himself think about the "to start out" part. He just grunted and made himself focus on the narrow task in front of him. What was actually in front of him was

Molly's slender back. He took the laces and eased them through the holes, his fingers brushing her soft skin with each move.

She shivered.

"Sorry." His fingers trembled. He was close enough that his breath could move the tendrils of hair at the nape of her neck. He wanted to kiss her there.

His breath hissed through his teeth in exasperation.

"Can't you get it?" Molly asked. She started to move away. "If it's too much trouble—"

"It's fine!" He held her still. Then when he was sure she was staying put, he poked a lace through the last hole and knotted them tightly together at the top, then stepped back and dropped his hands. "There."

She turned and smiled. "Thank you." But her eyes weren't smiling.

"You'll be fine," he told her gruffly. "Stop worrying."

"I'm not worrying." She was a lousy liar.

And he was a complete idiot for wanting to take her into his arms and tell her everything would be all right. So he shoved his hands in his pockets. "Is that all you need me for?"

She blinked. Started to say something, then stopped again. Silently she nodded.

"Fine. Have a good time, then." His tone was brusque, impatient. He didn't want to stand around and watch her leave with Sawyer. "I need to take a shower." He started for the stairs.

"Are you coming tonight? To the Wilsons'?"

"I'm going out to dinner. Meeting my folks at Beaches."

Did she want him to watch, for God's sake? Hell, maybe she did. Maybe she figured that if she needed pointers, she could run over and ask him, if he was there.

She smiled and said brightly, "Well, have a good time, then."

"I will."

Not.

HE STOPPED by Beaches on his way to the dock. His parents and Marianela and her mother were already at their table, and they looked surprised to see him in a formal dark suit and tie.

"I can't stay," he said, making his excuses. "I'm sorry. I thought I could be here, but I can't. I have…another obligation." There was no way to explain it. He couldn't explain it to himself.

He just knew he had to be there—to see her triumph? To see her success?

Was he that much of a masochist?

Maybe. He only knew he couldn't sit at Beaches and act polite and disinterested when the most important person in his life was seducing another man fifteen minutes away.

His mother looked disapproving, but his father said, "If you have an obligation, you must meet it. I hope," he added, "that we will see you in the morning, though. We are leaving tomorrow. I've had a fax from my colleague in New York. It has been a good holiday. But I must go home now. I have work to do."

"I'll see you in the morning," Joaquin promised. He let his gaze include all of them, even Marianela. After all, none of this was her fault.

Then he turned and walked swiftly out of the restaurant.

Tom Wilson had arranged launches to bring guests from Pelican Cay to the party.

"All you have to do is show up at the dock," Hugh had told him an hour ago when he'd called to see if they were going. "Tell 'em you're coming in my place. You're welcome. I don't go where I have to wear shoes unless they pay me."

Shoes were the least of Joaquin's problems. By the time he'd made up his mind to go, he wasn't going to let anything stand in his way.

He didn't have to tell anyone he was coming in Hugh's

place. He looked as if he fit right in. There were easily a couple of hundred people there when he arrived. All elegant. All formal. It looked more like a black tie reception on Paradise Island than a party on Pelican Cay. He could see why Molly would have felt daunted before. But he didn't doubt she'd be fine now. She had always had the gumption. She'd just needed the tools—or clothes—and the confidence to work with them.

Now she had them. And tonight she would show Carson she could manage very well in his world. Joaquin just wished he felt more of a sense of triumph and less one of hollow aching loss.

He ran into Nathan and Carin almost as soon as he got off the launch. They were delighted to see him, and if they were surprised they didn't say so.

"Come have a drink with us," Nathan said. "Have you seen this place? It's amazing."

Indeed it was. The house was a cross between something in a James Bond film and a rich beachcomber's fantasy. It was hard to say where it, with all its glass and native stone and cypress ended and the beach and foliage began. There was a swimming pool landscaped to look like a natural water hole. And paths led down from the house and terrace through low pines to small secluded decks where you could stand beneath the trees and overlook the gardens, the beach, the sea. A string quartet played dance music on the terrace. A few couples were dancing. And he looked, on his way to the bar with Nathan and Carin, to see if Molly was among them. She wasn't.

There were small groups of people everywhere Joaquin looked, but he didn't see Molly or Carson. Nathan handed him a beer and began telling him about a photo shoot a fashion photographer friend of his had done using Wilson's as the setting. Carin added details, and in another frame of mind, Joaquin would have found it entertaining.

But he was looking for Molly.

More people arrived. Some came up from walking on the beach. Others disappeared in that direction. A buffet was being served in the rooms above the terrace. He studied the people up there, trying—and failing—to pick out Molly.

"Getting hungry?" Nathan asked him.

He dragged his attention back to Nathan and Carin. "Not especially. But please go. I think I'll just go for a walk on the beach."

Nathan and Carin headed for the buffet. Joaquin circled the terrace, checking out all the people trying to be sure he hadn't missed her. He spotted David Grantham and a sultry-looking female who once would have been Joaquin's style. But tonight he barely even noticed her. Lachlan's assistant, Suzette, was dancing with a tall blond man he didn't know. She smiled in Joaquin's direction, and he returned it, but moved on.

Where the hell was she? How could she be convincing Carson that she could handle these sorts of occasions if she wasn't even here?

Unless it didn't matter. Unless they'd decided to skip it. Unless one look at Molly in her lace-up green-crayon wrapper and Carson had decided it would be more fun undressing the crayon and had taken her back to the Moonstone to do just that.

Joaquin's stomach clenched.

He turned around and bumped into Nathan's brother Dominic who was dancing with his wife, Sierra.

"Oh. Sorry." Joaquin apologized, stepping back.

"No problem," Dominic said easily. "Are you cutting in?"

"No!" Joaquin replied quickly, then realized that might be offensive to Sierra. "I mean, I'd like to dance with you, but—"

"Don't worry." Sierra patted his arm. "I don't expect you to. I'm only making Dominic dance with me as a penance for bringing work with him on our holiday." She grinned at her husband.

Dominic scowled. "You know I don't want to do it."

Sierra kissed his cheek. "I know." She was stunning in a hairstyle that seemed to be shot through with iridescent purple and burgundy and red. It was both memorable and flattering. But in Joaquin's estimation, it didn't hold a candle to the simplicity of Molly's natural red.

Speaking of which, was that her? he wondered as he caught sight of something red on the other side of the pool just past Sierra's left ear.

"If you'll excuse me," he said quickly, "I've seen someone I need to speak to."

He strode away, around the pool. But whatever—or whomever—he had seen, was gone. And there were so many places they could be in a place like this. The island was small, but the paths that snaked this way and that through the trees provided lots of little private secluded areas where a couple could go to be alone.

Joaquin wandered down one of them, looking here and there, and when he had his head turned once, almost stumbled into a couple in the throes of a passionate clinch.

For an instant he thought it was Molly and Carson. But the woman's hair was brown, not red, and she was nowhere near as lovely as Molly.

"Sorry," he muttered and, relieved, carried on up the path the way he'd come. He went back to the bar and got another beer, then wandered to the edge of the terrace and stood with the bottle dangling from his fingers while he stared across the trees to the sea and, in the distance, to the lights of Pelican Cay.

He might as well go back there. Molly wasn't here. And he didn't know what he'd have done if she had been. Had he planned to cheer at her social success or applaud her seduction of Carson?

It had been stupid to come. Pointless.

He took one last long pull on his beer and turned to go. And that was when he saw them.

They were almost directly below where he was standing, the two of them sitting on a bench in one of those secluded areas just off a path down to the beach. Joaquin's fingers tightened on the neck of the bottle as he eased closer to the edge of the terrace.

They were not kissing. They were touching. He could see Carson holding Molly's hands in his. Their heads were together. Their mouths barely inches apart. Their conversation was intent. And they had eyes only for each other.

Obviously the evening was a success.

He tried to find triumph. Henry Higgins had nothing on him.

He only felt sick.

He should have turned away. Should at least have shut his eyes and given them the privacy they'd sought when they'd chosen that secluded haven for their conversation.

But he couldn't. He couldn't move. He could only stare— and feel the pain.

It was what she wanted. Carson was the man she loved. He had known it from the beginning, hadn't he? Of course he had. But in the beginning it hadn't mattered because then he hadn't loved her.

And now he did.

It was that simple. And that hopeless.

The realization cut deep.

And then as Joaquin, oblivious to the music and conversation going on behind him, looked down on them, they stood up, her hand still in his. And then she loosed one hand and lifted it to Carson's cheek, stroking it lovingly. She smiled.

And then Carson's head bent and they kissed.

It was gentle. Tender. Exquisitely slow.

Exactly the way he'd taught her. And with every second that passed Joaquin felt the knife slide deeper inside him.

And then, finally, the kiss ended. Once more they smiled at each other.

Then, to Joaquin's astonishment, Carson walked away.

He turned and headed rapidly up the path. But Molly stayed where she was.

Perplexed, Joaquin watched as Carson reached the terrace, then crossed it and headed purposefully into the house. Moments later he came back out with a slender platinum blonde Joaquin recognized as Dena Wilson. They headed for the dock, but once they got beyond the trees, they disappeared from view.

Frowning, Joaquin turned back to look for Molly.

She hadn't moved. She stood quietly, staring into the distance. And then she started down the path toward the beach alone.

Unthinking, Joaquin went after her. By the time he got to the sand, she had her shoes in her hand and was ankle deep in the water, wearing her beautiful crayon dress.

And as he kicked off his own shoes, a Boston Whaler heading toward Pelican Cay came into view. In it were a dark-haired man and a woman with long platinum hair. Molly lifted her head and watched them go.

He came up behind her. "Molly?"

She whirled around. Her face was wet with tears.

"What happened?" he demanded. "What did he do to you?"

She swallowed and lifted her chin, but she didn't wipe away the tears. "He didn't do anything! We just…talked."

"Talked?"

"People do sometimes," she said sharply. "They don't just grab and take what they want."

His jaw clenched, but he didn't argue with her. "What happened?" he persisted quietly.

"We broke up." She laughed a little sadly. "Not that we had much breaking up to do. We weren't exactly hot and heavy, but we—" her voice wavered "—we loved each other for a long time. We still do. We just aren't…a couple." She cleared her throat and went on firmly, "He's in love with Dena. He thinks."

"He *thinks?*" Joaquin didn't know whether to be outraged or to cheer.

"He didn't want to be. He was engaged to me."

"And now he's dumped you and left with her?"

"He didn't *dump* me!"

"Of course he didn't," he said, though what the hell else you would call it, he didn't know.

"It isn't going to be easy for them. Her father isn't keen. He wants her to marry someone else. And Dena is used to doing what her father says."

Who the hell cared about Dena?

"What about you?" Joaquin demanded. "He was supposed to marry you!"

"I don't want to marry a man who doesn't love me! Not the way he ought to, at least. And…and anyway—" she hesitated "—I understand."

He supposed she did. He knew she wouldn't hold Carson to his commitment even though she loved him, because that's the sort of woman Molly was. She cared about everyone else before she cared about herself.

He reached down and took her hand. Her fingers jerked, then trembled. But she didn't pull them out of his grasp. They felt cold and dry, and he wanted to warm them. In the distance Carson's Boston Whaler had almost reached the harbor at Pelican Cay.

"Come on," Joaquin said.

They walked clear around the island. They didn't speak. They just walked. Every now and then he heard her draw a shaky breath. A sideways glance told him that fresh tears still glistened on her cheeks. They passed other couples but made no acknowledgment.

When they came to the dock, she drew her hand out of his, looked up at him and managed a faint smile. "Thank you."

He grunted, unable to trust his voice.

"I appreciate it," she went on. "I'm sure you'd have had

a far better time if you hadn't stumbled across me. Anyway, go back and enjoy the party. I'm going to go home now.''

"I'll come with you."

"You don't have to do that."

"I do." It was like a vow. One he'd never expected to say. But saying it, he knew it was true. There was nothing he had ever done in his life that he needed to do more than he needed to be with Molly now.

She was shivering as the launch started back across the water, so he took off his coat and put it around her shoulders. She smiled her thanks, but she didn't speak. They made the whole journey in silence. They walked back up the hill through Pelican Town to her place in silence, as well. There were plenty of people on the street, lots of whom they knew. Molly smiled and nodded at them, but she didn't stop.

Not until she was in her house with the door shut. And then she looked at him and said tremulously, "Thank you again. I seem to keep thanking you and thanking you. But now you've done enough."

Silently he reached out and took hold of the lapels of his coat, still resting on her shoulders and drew her closer. "No, I haven't," he whispered.

He only meant to erase her memory of Carson's kiss. He only meant to give her something else to think about tonight, the taste of someone else's mouth on hers to blot out the man she'd lost.

Or maybe he didn't. Maybe he'd always meant to go further. Always intended to do more.

God knew he'd been wanting to do more for days. He had been dying not to have to think about reining in his passion, dying to kiss her with all the need and desire and intensity he really felt.

And why not? She didn't belong to anyone else now. Except, of course, in her heart. In her heart, he knew, she was still Carson Sawyer's.

But for now—for tonight—Joaquin was determined to make her forget it.

The kiss went on, got hungrier, more desperate. Not just on his part, but on hers, as well. He could feel her heart beating faster, could feel the raggedness of her pulse, the tremor in her body pressed against his.

He wanted them upstairs before they went further. And he broke off the kiss. She looked at him, stunned.

"You don't—" she began.

He didn't know if she meant it to be a question or not. He only knew the answer.

"I do," he said gruffly and he swung her into his arms and carried her up the stairs. "I do," he said again, smiling at the words, getting the hang of them.

"Joaquin!" She wriggled, startled. "What are you—"

He silenced her with his lips and didn't release them until they were in her bedroom when he let her slide down so that she stood on her feet again. Then he turned her around, plucked his suit coat off her shoulders, tossed it aside and, with trembling fingers, tried to undo the knot at the nape of her neck. He'd tied it tightly to give Carson a bit of a challenge. Now he couldn't undo it himself.

"Damn it!" He bent his head and bit it in half with his teeth, and unlaced the rest with unbridled urgency. Then he turned her around again so she faced him and slowly he uncovered her beauty.

Molly, not to be outdone, went to work on the buttons of his shirt. Her fingers seemed much more agile than his. She had his buttons undone in seconds and was slipping his shirt from his shoulders, then running her hands over his chest. Her touch on his heated flesh made him tremble. He backed her toward the bed.

At the foot of it, she stopped and with a little shimmy slid right out of the crayon wrapper dress and stood before him in two scraps of lace. Were they the results of their shopping expedition? he wondered. Or had down-to-earth, sensible Molly always worn sexy underwear?

No time to think about it now. Only time to bear her back onto the bed and peel it off her. He shed his own trousers and shorts along the way, then lay alongside her, stroking the soft silk of her skin, no longer cold and dry, but warm and vibrant and alive.

It was interesting, he thought, when he could actually form a coherent thought, that Molly, who needed lessons in all the other stuff, didn't need lessons here.

She was not afraid. She was eager. She wasn't passive. She dared. She touched him as he touched her, giving as good as she got. And when he slipped between her legs and touched her intimately, she touched him back, caressed him, made him suck in his breath as she drew him down, wrapped him in her warmth and brought him home.

He couldn't think any more then. He could only feel. Only move. Only shatter as he felt her shatter beneath him. Only love.

He slumped, spent, against her and listened to their hearts galloping in unison. He buried his face against her neck and smelled the soft sea breeze and citrus that was so much a part of Molly. He clutched her close and didn't want to let her go.

He wanted to say, *There. See? It can be good for us. I can make it good. You can fall in love again. Didn't I make you forget? Didn't I?*

He felt something wet against his cheek and lifted his head and knew the answer before he even asked it because he saw her tears.

CHAPTER ELEVEN

SHE NEEDED A LESSON, Molly thought, in handling the morning after.

What did you do when a man made love to you for all the wrong reasons? What did you say when there was nothing suitable to say?

Nothing he would want to hear, at any rate.

Like protestations of undying love. He certainly wouldn't want to hear those, even though they were true.

Because the fact was, though Molly knew she loved Joaquin, she also knew he didn't love her. He had taken her to bed last night not because he loved her, but because he'd felt sorry for her.

He had seen her crying and concluded that she was distraught, when nothing could be further from the truth.

She had cried, yes. But not because she and Carson had ended an engagement that, in many respects, had never really begun. She was crying for the hopes and dreams that would never come to pass because the man she really loved didn't love her.

And how on earth could she tell him that?

She couldn't. She hadn't.

In fact, she had been every bit as pathetic as he'd believed her to be. She had welcomed his lovemaking, had relished every touch, had memorized them all to take out and remember for the rest of her days. And she hadn't even settled for making love with him once.

When she'd dozed off, snug in his embrace, she'd awakened to feel him quietly and carefully easing away. And she hadn't let him go. She had clung to him, run her hands over him, touched him.

One night, she'd told herself. Just one night. That was all she would ask for. Please God, one night of love wasn't too much.

And so he had stayed.

He had loved her again. This time his lovemaking had been less desperate. He had taken his time, moved more slowly, caressed more gently, but with no less passion, no less skill. He drew the experience out, as if to savor it. And Molly had certainly savored it, as well.

But now he was up and in the bathroom shaving. It was past eight and she knew he had to be at the soccer field before nine. She'd awakened when she missed his nearness, when she felt the mattress shift when he pulled away. It had taken all her willpower not to reach for him, to pull him back to love her again.

But her night of escape was over. The morning sun streamed through the window, welcoming her to the clear cold light of day.

She got up and pulled herself together, put on a pair of her new linen shorts and a gauzy cotton top that made her feel sexy even when she wasn't.

She didn't want him to feel sorry for her. She didn't want him to think of her as a charity case. She had more pride than that.

She went downstairs and put on coffee. He came down a few minutes later, looking lean and hard and gorgeous, his hair damp, his jaw smoothly shaved. He smiled at her, but his expression was wary, as if he were worried about what she might expect of him now.

But Molly didn't expect anything. She'd already had more than she had any right to expect from him. And so she smiled brightly and handed him a cup of coffee. "I can make you breakfast if you want," she offered.

"No, thanks. Gotta run. I—" He paused, as if unsure what to say. No doubt he was. Even a practiced lover like Joaquin Santiago probably didn't find himself in situations like this every day.

"Thank *you*," Molly said briskly and smiled. "You were very kind last night. And that was quite an education."

He looked surprised at her words, but he didn't reply. And in his silence she felt forced to continue.

"I learned a lot," she went on. "And I'm sure I'll have a use for it all," she added as flippantly and as cheerfully as she could manage, "when I'm ready to go back to playing the field."

THINKING OF MOLLY using their lovemaking as a basis for "playing the field" nearly made him lose it right there. He hung on to his control. Barely. And only because he knew her words were born out of pain.

She was miserable. She was missing that bastard Sawyer. And Joaquin wanted to kill the jerk for making Molly so unhappy. But at the same time he was glad that Sawyer was out of her life.

She was free. Available.

And someday, when she was over this…

And that was when reality kicked in. Someday, when she was over Carson Sawyer, he, Joaquin Santiago, would be in no better position to offer her a future than he was now.

His life was mapped out for him. He was going back to bloody Spain and dealing with the Santiago family business for the rest of his life. It was his duty. It always had been. And it was, as his father had long known, time to stop playing games and face it like a man.

"I'm leaving today," he told her.

"Leaving?"

"After the games." He shrugged. "My parents are leaving. And Marianela and her mother," he added. Then he shrugged as negligently as he could. "I might as well go, too. There's nothing to stay for now, is there?"

If he'd hoped she would say, yes! Me! he was doomed to disappointment.

She stood there, holding her coffee mug, looking absolutely blank. "Of course," she said slowly. "Of course, you're right. You had your holiday." Her gaze lifted and met his squarely. "And now you need to go home. To move on."

ALL DAY LONG she prayed it wouldn't happen. She watched him at the soccer games, running along the sidelines, exhorting the boys, encouraging, cheering. And she told herself he'd see the light, change his mind, realize his future was not in some dreary business half a world away. But even as she prayed, she knew that sometimes the answer you got wasn't the one you were hoping for.

And then the tournament was over. The Pelicans actually won.

"Of course we won," Lachlan said, as if he hadn't been biting his fingernails with worry and covering his eyes when things looked desperate. "You've just gotta have faith."

"And a good coach," Martin Santiago said. "Or two." He smiled at Lachlan and then over at his son who was on the other sideline being hugged and congratulated by parents and friends.

"He's a good man," Lachlan agreed. "We'll miss him."

"You will see him no doubt," Martin said. "He will take holidays. He will come visit. He will not forget Pelican Cay. He will bring his family someday."

"He'd better," Lachlan said gruffly.

Molly just listened and ached. She was glad no one talked to her. She couldn't have said anything at all.

She didn't want to stand there and watch him leave. But she had to. She had spent too many years dreaming foolish dreams about Carson and her because she couldn't face the reality that was staring her in the face. She needed to face this reality.

And so she stood in the shed and watched as the Santiagos and Marianela and her mother all got in Hugh's helicopter. Joaquin was the last one aboard. He hugged Syd and Fiona and Lachlan. He clapped the boys on the shoulder. And then he paused and looked around.

For her?

Perhaps. She would hope so. But she couldn't go out there. It was too hard. There was a limit to how much control any one woman could be expected to have. So she stayed in the shop and watched out the window as Joaquin, with one last look, climbed into the chopper and the door shut.

The people on the field backed away, and Hugh started the engine. It kicked up clouds of dust and whipped everyone's shirts and dresses before, slowly and inexorably, it lifted off the field, hovered a moment, then turned and moved away, taking with it her heart.

She stood and watched and faced reality until she couldn't see it anymore. And then she went back to the Jeep and dripped tears onto the hot manifold and watched them hiss.

BARCELONA WAS much as he had left it. Huge. Crowded. Noisy. Filled with diesel fumes and car exhaust and an energy and a cosmopolitan charm he'd forgotten.

He didn't care. He barely noticed.

His mother fussed over him, delighted he was home, telling him that it was all right if he didn't fancy Marianela. She was a lovely young woman, but there were others. Lots of others. He could take his pick.

I want Molly. He thought the words but didn't say them. Couldn't even say her name, though he thought about her night and day.

"You are too quiet," his mother complained. "Are you getting sick?"

"I'm fine, Mama," he told her with as earnest a smile as

he could manage. "I'm just getting settled in. Jet lag takes a while."

His mother didn't look convinced. And since she'd bounced right back from her jet lag, she found his suspect. He didn't blame her.

"Take a day to sleep," his father suggested. "You can have tomorrow off. I'd take it myself but I have things to do."

"No," Joaquin declined firmly. "If you have things to do, I do, too."

Martin gave him a long look, which Joaquin met steadily. He was here and he was ready to meet his responsibilities. But he shook his head. "I'll be there in the morning. Begin as you mean to go on and all that."

Martin looked sceptical.

"Papa, I'll be there. I didn't come all the way home to back out now."

He was there, as promised, bright and early in the morning. He was emotionally no more enthused than ever. But he was determined. He thought he was doing a pretty good job of it, too, even though he was there on his own because his father had meetings and couldn't be there to show him around.

Well, so what? He'd been here before, although not for years. And he knew his father had obligations. It was better this way, he decided. It let him get his feet wet on his own.

It let him stand at the window, staring out at the city, thinking not about mergers and expansions but about Molly McGillivray. He was startled when the phone on his desk rang. He picked it up.

"Ah. So you are there. Will you come with me for lunch?" his father asked.

For a workaholic like Martin, the correct answer was probably no, thanks. I'll eat at my desk.

"Go out for lunch?" Joaquin asked warily.

"We need to talk," Martin said.

Ah, yes. The "how glad I am you finally came to your

senses'' lecture. His father had probably spent the morning polishing it.

"All right. Where?''

"Te espero en Tibidabo,'' Martin said, confounding him.

Why on earth would his father be at Tibidabo? An amusement park, among other things, high on a hill overlooking the city, it was a place for families and holiday outings. Not a place for business discussions.

Joaquin hadn't been there in years. It took him two buses, the *tramvia blau* and the funicular to get to the top of the hill. It was an adventure just making the trip.

The whole thing was crazy, Joaquin thought. And very unlike his father. Had the old man got too much sun on Pelican Cay? Maybe he was losing his mind. Maybe it was a very good thing he had come home to take over now.

He worried all the way to the top, half expecting to see a confused shadow of the man he had seen just this morning at breakfast.

But Martin looked strong and lively and healthy as he came to meet him. He was beaming and took Joaquin by the arm, saying, *"Ven.* Come along. Let's have a coffee first and sit here.''

He bought them each small *cortados,* strong coffee with milk, and they sat at a small table overlooking the city. It was hazy today. Not beautiful as it was sometimes on days when the wind had blown the fumes and smog and dust out to sea.

Not beautiful as it was every day on Pelican Cay. His throat tightened and ached as he tried to shove the thought away. To appreciate Barcelona. To listen to his father. To get on with the rest of his life.

Martin sipped his coffee and looked out across the city. "I come here,'' his father said, "whenever I need to see the big picture.''

Joaquin nodded. Here it came. He settled back against the rusty wrought iron of the chair and tried to look attentive.

"I come to see the future,'' his father went on. "To think

about my part in it. Your part in it. Santiagos, the business's part in it. I see more than just what I want to see in front of me then. At least—" he smiled a little wryly "—I hope that I do."

Joaquin waited patiently for his father to get to the point.

"Sometimes a different perspective makes all the difference." Martin stared into his cup and then out into the distance again. "Whether from here or from New York or from Pelican Cay. It is a lovely place." He smiled thoughtfully and stirred his coffee.

Joaquin swallowed. "Yes."

"You were alive there." Martin looked at him suddenly, nailed him with his gaze.

Joaquin straightened. The wrought iron poked him in the back. "I'm alive here," he retorted.

His father nodded. "But not happy. Soccer makes you happy. Santiagos never will."

"You don't know—" Joaquin began.

But his father cut him off. "I do know. I know a man must do what he loves. And I loved this business. I woke up every morning eager to come to work, eager to try new things, eager to learn more, to build, to grow."

The energy in him was obvious. Joaquin could hear it in his voice, see it in the light in his eyes.

Martin's voice dropped. "I wanted that for you."

"I'm here," Joaquin reminded him. The last thing he needed right now was criticism for doing what was expected of him.

"Yes." Martin leaned back in his own chair and smiled. "Because I asked you. No, I demanded. And you are a good son. You said yes. You tried to be what I wanted."

Joaquin didn't say anything to that. He didn't know where his father was going. He didn't know what to say.

"I am retiring," Martin told him.

"Not yet!" Joaquin leaned forward urgently. "You can't

retire yet. I don't know the first damned thing about running the business."

"And with luck you will never have to," his father said. His dark eyes were smiling.

Joaquin stared at him. "What are you talking about?"

"You doing what you love to do. What you tried for years to get me to understand. You play soccer."

"I can't play anymore!" Joaquin almost yelled at him.

"But you still love it. And you can coach. You do coach. Very well. I have seen you."

"I barely did anything," Joaquin muttered. He slumped back against the wrought iron again.

"But you loved it," his father said confidently. "You would like to do it some more. Yes?"

Joaquin shrugged. "I suppose."

Martin laughed. "I suppose, too, *mi hijo*. And so I have seen the light. I have agreed to a merger with my friend in New York. The one with the sons."

"Who work with him," Joaquin added grimly.

"Two of whom work with him," his father corrected. "The third does something with rocket science, I believe. He loves it." He was still smiling, looking very satisfied with himself. "We will still own as much as we own now. But my friend and his sons will be active. I will retire, and come and visit my son on Pelican Cay."

"I'm not—"

"Perhaps not." Martin shrugged lightly. "I do not make decisions for you anymore. You will follow your heart, Joaquin. It is the only way."

IF THE PAST FEW DAYS had been the first days of the rest of her life, Molly dared to hope that today wouldn't be as awful.

Yesterday there had been no Joaquin. No lessons.

Only work. Change the spark plugs. Plug the leak. Drain the radiator. Change the oil. Nothing to look forward to.

And more of the same today.

Hugh had taken the sea plane to Nassau to pick up some tourists who'd decided at the last minute they would like to visit Pelican Cay. Probably they'd heard about it from people who'd attended the festival.

According to David Grantham, who ought to know, Pelican Cay was now a "first-class tourist destination." They were, according to David, a thriving place. "The world will be beating a path to your doorstep," he told them.

Which Molly supposed would be nice, if she wanted to stay. She loved it here. But everywhere she looked now, she remembered Joaquin there. She couldn't walk past the Moonstone or look out the window at the soccer field or have a beer in the Grouper. She couldn't even go to bed at night without remembering, "Joaquin was here."

She needed a change. Maybe tomorrow she should ask Hugh to let her do one of the charters. Ordinarily she did them only when he was otherwise occupied. Ordinarily she was perfectly happy working on her engines.

At least she had been B.J.

Before Joaquin.

Someday she would again, she promised herself. It would take time, but she would get over it. Someday.

But now she had to check out the fuel line leak in Lachlan's truck. She lay back on the roller and maneuvered herself underneath it. She hung the shop light where she could examine the line and began to use her heels to squirm along, propelling herself.

She heard footsteps. Turned her head and saw a pair of male feet in deck shoes. "I'll be with you in a minute," she said. "If you want to go somewhere today, my brother's in Nassau. I'm the only one who can take you."

"You'll do."

The voice was so familiar and so completely unexpected that she sat up. "Ow!" She fell back, seeing stars, disbelieving.

But he was on his knees in an instant, peering underneath

the truck, grabbing her by the ankles and yanking her out from beneath it. "My God, *querida,* are you all right?"

Molly rubbed her forehead where a good-size egg was forming. "I…don't—" she was going to say *know.* She said "—believe it." She stared at him, doubting her perceptions. But he was lifting her now, touching her! Pulling her toward him and brushing her hair gently away from the goose egg on her head.

"We'll call the doctor," he said.

"We will not," Molly contradicted at once. "I'm fine. I banged my head. You made me bang my head, sneaking up on me like that. Where did you come from? What are you doing here?"

He looked tired and unshaven and absolutely wonderful. "I came from Barcelona. I came to see you. I—" and then he stopped, drew in a ragged breath and raked his fingers through his hair.

Don't stop now! Molly wanted to shout at him. She couldn't take her eyes off him. She opened her mouth, but she found she couldn't speak, either, couldn't demand to know what had changed, why he was back.

Slowly, starting from the beginning, he told her. He told her about his father retiring. He told her about a place called Tibidabo and a view of the future and a change of perspective and a whole lot of things that probably would make sense if she could just get past thinking over and over, *He's here! He's here!*

"So you don't have to work for him?" She cut to the bottom line.

"I don't have to work for him."

"Then…what *do* you have to do?" She couldn't believe he didn't have to do something.

A corner of his mouth twisted. "Follow my heart, *querida.*"

She stared at him, unspeaking, unable to say a word, her breath caught in her throat.

He lowered his gaze for a moment, then lifted it again and met hers. "I know it's too soon. I know you still love Carson. I don't expect that to change. Not yet. But someday—" he said the words almost urgently, and he caught her grimy hands in his "—someday, Molly, you will. I promise you. Someday you'll be ready to try again, to play the field and—"

"I don't want to play the field."

The light went out of his eyes. His expression grew grim. His shoulders slumped like a man defeated. She had never ever seen Joaquin Santiago defeated.

"I don't want to play the field," she repeated. "I want you."

His head jerked up. He stared at her, incredulous. Ran his tongue over his lips. "You…what?"

"You heard me. I don't want to play the field. I'm not interested. Never will be. I love Carson—" the light that had come back flickered again, and she realized for the first time how much she meant to him, how badly she could hurt him if she weren't careful "—but not the way you think I love him."

He just looked at her.

"I love him like I love Lachlan and Hugh. Like a brother. I told him that the night of the Wilsons' party."

"You told *him?*"

Molly nodded. "It wasn't him dumping me. It turned out we'd both been giving things a lot of thought. You know what I was thinking—" She grinned.

"That you wanted to marry him and have his babies," Joaquin said darkly.

"Sort of. I wanted to get married and have kids. Carson was my fiancé. Who else was I supposed to be thinking about?"

"Me," he said, pure arrogance.

She laughed. "I was," she admitted. "Not at first. But it didn't take long."

"You wanted him. You were crying when he left."

"For all the dreams we'd had as kids that would never be. But mostly I was crying because of you."

"Me?" He wasn't arrogant now, only shocked.

"I loved you and that was about as hopeless as it could get!"

"Hopeless?" He was beyond shocked now and into thunderstruck.

"You weren't ever getting married."

"Who said that?" he demanded.

"You did. Lots of times."

"Oh." He had the grace to flush. "Well, that was then. That was when groupies and Mama's perfect Santiago brides were the only candidates. You can't blame me for not wanting them."

"And now?"

Joaquin shook his head. His eyes glistened and his smile was equal parts tender and bemused. "Now I love you, and I'd go down on one knee—if I wasn't already sitting on the floor—and I'd ask you to marry me."

Molly stared at him. "Really?"

"Really." He grinned at her, then pressed a gentle kiss to the bump on her forehead. He would kiss all her bumps and bruises for years to come if only she would let him. "Do you need a lesson in how to answer that question, Ms. McGillivray?"

Slowly, smiling, laughing, crying, Molly shook her head.

"There is only one answer to that question, *amor mio*. And the answer is yes." And she took his face between her grease-spattered hands and gave him forever in her kiss.

THERE WERE three hammocks strung among the palm trees overlooking Pelican Cay's pink sand beach. There was a barefoot pregnant woman swaying gently in each.

"This is the life," Fiona said, sipping pineapple soda and stretching lazily as she smiled across at her sisters-in-law.

"*You* can say that," Sydney groaned. "You aren't as big

as a whale." She patted her considerable belly. "Nor are you being kicked to death by a legion of battling Scots."

"Not a legion," Molly corrected from her own hammock where she had been lying ever since the dinner her husband and brothers had cooked. "You're only having two."

Boys, the ultrasound had showed. Boys who would be named Alastair and Iain when they arrived sometime in the next six weeks. Hugh had already announced that he was taking Syd to the mainland soon, not wanting to take any risks if the babies should come early.

"Life is a risk," Syd had argued, but the look Hugh had given her said this was one battle she wasn't going to win. Now she rubbed at a sudden foot-shaped bulge kicking out from her abdomen, then rolled onto her side to look at Molly, her gaze narrowing. "What do you mean, 'only'?"

Trust Syd. All her years in business had taught her to hear and probe the meaning of every single word. Molly wriggled a little in the hammock, still a little shell-shocked herself at the news she'd got this afternoon at her own ultrasound. "We're having three."

"Three?" Both Fiona and Syd struggled up and gaped at her.

"You're joking." Fiona said. "Tell me you're joking. For *your* sake, you'd better be joking!"

"She's not joking." Joaquin came down the steps from the broad front porch of the house they'd built over the past year, scooped his wife up into his arms and smiled down at her with a look of such love that Molly felt a lump grow in her throat. It was a look she never got tired of, just as she would never tire of the man.

"Three?" Hugh said with a wary grin. "Is this another one of those 'anything they can do I can do better' things?" He reached out and ruffled his sister's short hair.

"If it is," Lachlan said with the voice of weary experience, "they'll soon have triple the number of sleepless nights. Lucky them," he added with a grin. He reached down and hauled a sand-eating redheaded toddler into his arms, rubbing noses with him and grinning. "But they'll grow out of it. You sleep through the night now, don't you, Dunc, ol' buddy?"

Duncan giggled and gurgled and pulled his father's hair, bouncing in his arms and saying, "Da! Dad! 'Wim!'"

Lachlan understood at once. "Sure we'll go swimming. And you, my lady?" he asked holding out a hand to Fiona, who let him haul her to her feet and slid an arm around his waist.

"Coming?" Lachlan asked the rest of them.

"Absolutely." Syd held out her hands to Hugh. "Water is the one place where being a whale isn't a disadvantage."

"You're the most beautiful whale in the world," Hugh vowed. When he had her on her feet and steady, he pressed two kisses to her belly and one to her lips, then turned to Joaquin and Molly. "What about you? You guys coming?"

"Of course." Molly started to roll out of the hammock, determined to do everything as long as her body was still her own.

"Not now," Joaquin said, waving them away.

"You're not going to get all overprotective and pesky now, are you?" Molly challenged him, turning her attention from her brothers and their wives to the man she loved.

"What do you think?"

She rolled her eyes and grinned impishly. "I think you'll be bossy and dictatorial and never give me a minute's peace for the next six months."

"How perceptive of you, *querida*." A grin slashed across his face. Then just as abruptly it vanished. "Three babies," he murmured. *"Tres niños."* He wiped a hand over his face. "Terrifying."

Molly took a deep breath. "It is," she agreed. "But exciting."

"Yeah, but are we up for it?" he wondered.

"We are." Molly was positive. She laced her fingers through his, then leaned up to kiss him. It was a scorching kiss. By the time she was done, even the tips of his ears were red. "See? I couldn't do that eighteen months ago, could I?"

He made a strangled noise.

She laughed. "So, there is no end to the things we can learn if we put our minds to them. Come on. Let's swim while we still have time for each other."

She tried to tow him toward the water, but found herself scooped up into his arms and carried instead.

"We will always have time for each other, *querida*," he promised her. "And as for what Lachlan said, I figure we're already old hands at that."

Molly blinked. "Old hands?"

Joaquin grinned and kissed her lingeringly as he reminded her, "We've already had some very enjoyable sleepless nights."

Michelle Reid's
THE PURCHASED WIFE
on sale June 2005, #2470

Your dream ticket to the love affair of a lifetime!

Why not relax and allow Harlequin Presents®
to whisk you away to stunning international
locations with our miniseries…

*Where irresistible men and sophisticated women
surrender to seduction under the golden sun.*

**Don't miss this opportunity to experience
glamorous lifestyles and exotic settings!**

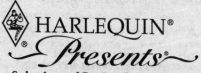

Seduction and Passion Guaranteed!

www.eHarlequin.com

HPTPW

If you enjoyed what you just read,
then we've got an offer you can't resist!

Take 2 bestselling love stories FREE!

Plus get a FREE surprise gift!

Clip this page and mail it to **Harlequin Reader Service®**

IN U.S.A.
3010 Walden Ave.
P.O. Box 1867
Buffalo, N.Y. 14240-1867

IN CANADA
P.O. Box 609
Fort Erie, Ontario
L2A 5X3

YES! Please send me 2 free Harlequin Presents® novels and my free surprise gift. After receiving them, if I don't wish to receive anymore, I can return the shipping statement marked cancel. If I don't cancel, I will receive 6 brand-new novels every month, before they're available in stores! In the U.S.A., bill me at the bargain price of $3.80 plus 25¢ shipping & handling per book and applicable sales tax, if any*. In Canada, bill me at the bargain price of $4.47 plus 25¢ shipping & handling per book and applicable taxes**. That's the complete price and a savings of at least 10% off the cover prices—what a great deal! I understand that accepting the 2 free books and gift places me under no obligation ever to buy any books. I can always return a shipment and cancel at any time. Even if I never buy another book from Harlequin, the 2 free books and gift are mine to keep forever.

106 HDN DZ7Y
306 HDN DZ7Z

Name _____ (PLEASE PRINT)

Address _____ Apt.# _____

City _____ State/Prov. _____ Zip/Postal Code _____

Not valid to current Harlequin Presents® subscribers.

Want to try two free books from another series?
Call 1-800-873-8635 or visit www.morefreebooks.com.

* Terms and prices subject to change without notice. Sales tax applicable in N.Y.
** Canadian residents will be charged applicable provincial taxes and GST.
   All orders subject to approval. Offer limited to one per household.
   ® are registered trademarks owned and used by the trademark owner and or its licensee.

PRES04R   ©2004 Harlequin Enterprises Limited

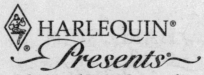

Introducing a brand-new trilogy by

Sharon Kendrick

Passion, power and privilege—the dynasty
continues with these handsome princes…

THE

Royal House

OF

Cacciatore

Welcome to Mardivino—a beautiful and
wealthy Mediterranean island principality,
with a prestigious and glamorous royal family.
There are three Cacciatore princes—Nicolo,
Guido and the eldest, the heir, Gianferro.

This month (May 2005) you can meet Nico in
THE MEDITERRANEAN
PRINCE'S PASSION #2466

Next month (June 2005) read Guido's story in
THE PRINCE'S LOVE-CHILD #2472

Coming in July: Gianferro's story in
THE FUTURE KING'S BRIDE #2478

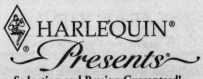

HARLEQUIN®
Presents

Seduction and Passion Guaranteed!

www.eHarlequin.com   HPRHOC

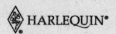